The Hangman's Master

ELYSE HOFFMAN

ISBN (ebook): 978-1-952742-34-7
ISBN (paperback): 978-1-952742-35-4
ISBN (hardcover): 978-1-952742-36-1

Project 613 Publishing
elysehoffman.com

PROJECT613

While "*The Hangman's Master*" can be enjoyed as a standalone story, it is also a continuation of Elyse Hoffman's previous book, ***Adiel and the Führer.*** Characters and plot details from ***Adiel and the Führer*** might be referenced in this book.

You might enjoy this story more if you read ***Adiel and the Führer*** first.

Thank you, and enjoy!

Adiel and
the Führer

ELYSE HOFFMAN

Chapter

ONE

The day that Stefan Harkel became a God was five years after he left the Nazi Party, one year after he joined the resistance, two months after Hitler's invasion of Poland, and one hour after he found his first mass grave.

"Piss, shit, fuck..." he whispered, covering his nose. Stefan had seen dead bodies before. Dead bodies of Brownshirt troopers murdered by their fellow Nazis during the Night of Long Knives. Dead bodies in Dachau the first, second, and third time he had been arrested for subversive activities. Plenty of dead bodies since he and the rest of his troop had started traversing Eastward in search of Jews to rescue.

Stefan had seen dead bodies before, but never so many, and never so young.

"Shit, shit, shit..." Stefan whispered, leaning over the pit, nausea filling his body as he gazed at the corpses. Flies flitted across dead toddlers' cheeks, dried blood clung to old ladies' hair, babies lay at the top of the pile, torn to shreds by bullets.

The Nazi *Einsatzgruppen* forces had previously targeted men for their massacres. Jewish men, Polish men, communist men, but always men.

Either the *Einsatzgruppen* unit that had come by this village had gone rogue or, more likely, Adolf Hitler's orders had changed. Broadened. Now all Jews were on the chopping block, from the fighting-aged man to the newborn baby.

There was evil, which the Nazis had undoubtedly been before, but then there was this. This went beyond the realm of evil. Stefan had not possessed many doubts about his fight against the Nazi Reich, about whether or not turning against his own nation was just, but now the few doubts he'd had vanished. These child-murderers were irredeemable, and when he got his hands on them…

"Five…Black Fox Five?"

Between the shock and the fact that he still wasn't quite used to the anti-Nazi Black Fox group's practice of using code numbers to refer to one another in place of names, Stefan, a.k.a. Black Fox Five, almost didn't hear his comrade's tepid voice. He turned and nodded at the wide-eyed Black Fox Fifteen.

"What do we do?" Fifteen said. "Can we give them a proper burial?"

"No, we don't have time," Stefan replied, even though saying that they *didn't have time* to bury a pit full of toddlers made his mouth taste sour. "If we stop to give everyone a proper burial, there are going to be more graves."

"We can't just leave them like this…" another Black Fox who was probably too young to be fighting Nazis said. "Can't we at least…bury them? Say Kaddish?"

"Put up a stone or something?" someone else suggested, his voice trembling with anger. Stefan gritted his teeth, unleashed a shuddering breath, and almost said something awful like: *Why bother with a gravestone when they're all dead and nobody's left to visit it?* He chastised himself for thinking something so morbid and nodded.

It took longer than he would have liked to cover the corpses with dirt, carve one word of Hebrew into a nearby stone, and for the Jews in the party of Black Foxes to chant.

"Yitgadal v'yitkadash sh'mei raba…"

The Jews prayed while Stefan and the gentiles hung back, all doffing their hats. Stefan's chest roiled with anger. A part of him wanted so badly to yell at them: *Why are you wasting time praying to a God that either doesn't exist or doesn't give a shit about you when we could be saving children?*

Saying all of that would have been horribly insensitive, however. Maybe the Jewish Black Foxes would fight harder thinking that there was something waiting for them in the afterlife. That there was a loving, just God watching over them. Screeching his own well-founded atheistic beliefs would only sow discord between the Jews and gentiles in their troop.

Besides, the Nazis were trying so hard to extinguish anything and everything Jewish, from the people themselves to their traditions and beliefs. If there was still one person saying these stupid, useless Hebrew prayers after the war was over, then Adolf Hitler would be a failure.

Stefan's troop kept moving after the makeshift funeral. There was silence amongst the Black Foxes, save for the occasional murmur of vengeful comfort from gentile to Jew. *We'll get them. We'll stop them. We'll make them pay for this.*

And that was the only thing that kept Stefan going, that kept him from wanting to curl up against the nearest evergreen, vomit his guts out, and just stop breathing. A fire in his chest, a melding of anger and guilt and something else. A desire to hunt down those animals wearing human flesh and rip their skin from their bones, their eyes from their skulls, their heads from their bodies. *Make them fucking pay.*

"Five, do you think we should—?"

Stefan's comrade was cut off with a suddenness that would have normally meant someone had slit his throat. Stefan put his hand on his sidearm and turned to find that his troop was fine. Untouched. Unmoving.

The Black Foxes stood about like a picture made flesh, a moment in time captured, some frozen in impossible positions, one of them literally floating as he hopped over a large log. The wind had stopped, the distant hum of bombers had stopped, time itself had stopped.

"What the Hell…?" was all Stefan could say, trying to decide whether he was going mad, or had died somehow, maybe of a spontaneous heart attack, and the afterlife was stranger than he could have imagined.

"Stefan Harkel."

A voice, a strangely familiar voice, like the voice of a relative he hadn't seen since he was small. Male, young, and tinged with an arrogant lilt that Stefan had only heard in Gestapo interrogation chambers.

Stefan turned again and aimed his gun at the stranger, the only lifeform besides himself that continued to move. A figure bedecked in a black cloak and hood, with black gloves and boots to match, stood in his path. In the center of the stranger's chest was a golden triangle that pointed downwards, and covering his face was a strange mask fashioned from a curved mirror. Stefan aimed at his own distorted reflection, and the figure chuckled.

"Do not bother," the stranger said. "It won't work."

Stefan pulled on the trigger, and indeed, nothing happened, not even the resistance of a jam. It was like his gun had been rendered a useless toy.

The stranger drew closer and spoke again. "The fire

of righteous justice burns in your soul. The Court of Heaven demands your service."

There was quite a lot in that sentence that Stefan could have questioned, but his ever-rebellious spirit settled on: "*Demands?*"

The stranger chuckled and crossed his arms over his triangle-emblazoned chest like a mummified Pharaoh, offering the Black Fox a small bow.

"Allow me to introduce myself," he said. "I am Ha-Satan. The Archangel of Justice, the Prosecutor of the Heavenly Court, and the Chief of the Heavenly Board of Punishment and Purification."

Crazy. Okay, Stefan was going crazy. He didn't feel crazy, but maybe that was how it worked. Maybe drooling nutcases also thought that they were just in the middle of a frozen moment in time being introduced to Satan.

Ha-Satan spoke again, this time using a gently commanding voice, like he was speaking to a very stupid toddler. "I realize you might have heard quite a bit about me. I assure you that it is all false. I am not a fallen angel. I loyally serve the Creator of the universe and happily fulfill my purpose."

"Well..." Stefan said at last, his tone hoarse. "Isn't that the sort of thing the Devil would say?"

Ha-Satan chuckled, and it felt like the air trembled when he did so. "I suppose. I rarely bother approaching Christians for this very reason. They rarely trust me. But you're a reasonable man..."

"A reasonable man wouldn't be talking to a...whatever you are," Stefan stuttered, feeling his knees wobble. "It's more likely that I had a psychotic break because I saw a fucking pit full of dead kids and now I'm *crazy*."

Stefan's voice broke a bit, and he stared at his own reflection in the angel's mirror mask. For a fraction of a second, he could swear he saw the mass grave in the mask, but then Ha-Satan tilted his head sideways and Stefan saw only his own distorted, panicked countenance.

"Yes. You've had a long day." The angel's voice was filled with genuine empathy. "Please...rest assured, those children are well cared for. I see to that myself. The innocent should be rewarded and protected. The guilty who harm them, however, should get what they deserve. *Ain takhat ain.* An eye for an eye."

Maybe that was the exact sort of thing the Satan that Stefan's mother had feared would say, but Stefan, who had never believed anything she spouted about God or the Devil, slowly nodded. "I...ah...know a Rabbi in the Black Foxes. I think he mentioned that Jews don't believe Satan's a demon. He said he was more like...a lawyer."

"Many would say that's apples to apples," Ha-Satan joked, and Stefan couldn't help but give a little chuckle. "Regardless, he wasn't entirely wrong. As I said, I am the Prosecuting Angel. When a soul sins, I record their sin. When they arrive in Judgment, I present their sins and make the case against them. Most of the time, souls only receive minor punishments. A few years or even minutes in Purgatory to cleanse their souls."

Slowly, Satan turned away from the Black Fox, crossing his arms behind his back and gazing out at the horizon, at the blood-red sunset frozen like a painting. "But sometimes...sometimes there is no washing away their evil. Sometimes, I win a case. Tell me, Herr Harkel, what do you think should happen to wicked men when they die?"

That seemed like a lawyer question, the sort of thing that Stefan sensed he should answer as vaguely as possible. He settled on shrugging.

"I may not be the Devil, Herr Harkel, but I *am* in charge of Hell," Ha-Satan explained, slowly pacing towards the Black Fox, not quite circling Stefan but giving off the air that he was, like a shark trying to decipher if a swimmer was a meal or merely a hunk of driftwood. "However, there is a difference between humans and angels. You humans were made in the image of God. That means you share a unique quality with Him—*creativity*. This is something angels lack. Something *I* lack. So punishing the wicked in a way that they deserve is difficult for an angel. And so, long ago, I had an idea..."

Ha-Satan found a stump from a tree felled either by a lumberjack that had abandoned his craft during the invasion or a bomb. The angel sat on it, stretching his gloved hands towards the frozen Black Foxes. "You humans enlist one another into your court system for your juries, so why not do the same thing? Enlist humans to oversee the punishment of the wicked. And so, I divided Hell into a series of different Zones, and in each Zone, I've placed a certain number of souls—in this one five, in that one five hundred. The worst of the worst. Murderers, rapists, the sinners who have lost the right to their own free will. And then...I give their souls over to a human, just like you. You get to become their warden, their Master, their new God."

With a flourish of one gloved hand, the angel summoned a glistening yellow triangle about the size of his palm. Ha-Satan beckoned for Stefan to come close. Stefan obeyed, driven by curiosity (and the fact that his mother would have *fainted* if she knew he was about to accept something from Satan himself.)

Stefan took the triangle and discovered that it was a folded-up piece of paper. At Ha-Satan's urging, he unfolded it.

One page typed in a gothic font. At the very top was an insignia: an upside-down yellow triangle inside a black circle. Under the triangle was a motto in red script.

HELL IS MERCY

Beneath that, more gothic script in black ink:

**THE LORD HAS GIVEN THEE
A POWER KNOWN TO ONLY HE
THE POWER OF COMPLETE CONTROL
OVER THIS, A HUMAN SOUL
UNTIL THE MOMENT OF REPENTANCE
AND THE END OF THEIR SENTENCE
THE ONE WHO SIGNS THIS
CONTRACT
IS HEREBY THE MASTER OF
ZONE N-74
AND THE FOLLOWING SOULS CONFINED THEREIN**

There was a list of about fifteen names beneath the poem, none of which were familiar to Stefan. Something about the silver script they were written in was…odd. When Stefan ran his fingers along the names, it was like touching a live animal. He could practically feel the thrum of a heartbeat.

"Some of the *Einsatzgruppen* soldiers who carried out that massacre," Ha-Satan explained when Stefan looked up, and this time the Black Fox was *certain* that he saw the mass grave they had found in the angel's mirror mask. "They met with some trouble on their way to another slaughter. Ambushed by partisans. You won't be able to give them what they deserve in this life, but as their Master…"

With another wave of his hand, Ha-Satan summoned a pen. The angel offered it to Stefan. "As their Master, you can do whatever you want to them. You will be the God of their Zone, and the sinners will become your Subjects. The Zone will be a small universe, and you can mold it to be whatever you wish in order to punish your Subjects. You could strand them on a planet of fire. You could make them forget they're dead and concoct some scenario to make them miserable. Or...you could use a **Command**."

There was a sinisterness to the way the angel said the seemingly innocuous word that made a shiver go up Stefan's spine. "Command?"

"The Creator, above all, values free will," explained Ha-Satan brusquely. "But God does not see what goes on in the Zones of Hell. As punishment for the sinners' evil crimes, He has turned His eye away from them. You are all they have, and you have complete and utter control. You can make them do whatever you want with just a word. Force your will upon them."

Stefan's jaw tightened, and he stared down at the fifteen names. A Hans here, a Helmut there. He wondered what they looked like. He wondered how they had felt when they were using their free will to shoot babies in the skull.

Maybe it was all a trick. Maybe signing a document offered by Satan was a dumb fucking idea.

But it would be worth it for a chance to grab those monsters' souls and *twist* them.

Stefan took the pen and signed the paper. A strange feeling swept through his body as he finished off the final 'l': a rush of adrenaline, a sensation of power that was as frightening as it was intoxicating. A familiar feeling, that: one he hadn't experienced since shedding his Nazi uniform for the last time.

"Very good," said Ha-Satan. "Now, the Manual will be in the Master Room. I recommend you read it."

"Master Room?" repeated Stefan, gazing down at the Contract. "Wait, now what? What do I do? How do I use this?"

"It's easy enough," Ha-Satan said. "Just think that you want to enter the Zone and you'll be there. And don't worry: if your body is disturbed, you'll be brought back out."

"B-body, what?"

"Your soul goes into the Zone, Herr Harkel, not your whole body. It would be rather suspicious if you suddenly disappeared. Do be careful if you have some important object on you; sentimental things sometimes follow you down."

"Wait, what?"

"—stop and set up camp?"

But when Stefan looked up, Ha-Satan was gone, and time was no longer standing still. Stefan turned to Black Fox Fifteen and tried to feign sanity.

"Err…yeah, sure. Camp," Stefan muttered, folding up the Contract into a triangle. He realized rather quickly as they ducked off the road and started setting up camp for the night that none of his comrades could see the little slip of paper—at one point, Black Fox Ninety-Four asked her commander why he kept staring at his hands.

He also learned that he couldn't put the Contract down. In fact, he got a rather unpleasant surprise when he tried to drop it. As soon as Stefan released his grip on the Contract, it flew right at him, sticking to his chest just above his heart and scaring the absolute shit out of him in the process. (His poor comrades ended up wasting a couple of bullets on the trees, thinking that Black Fox Five had been shot by a Nazi in the shadows.)

After he calmed down his comrades, convincing them that he'd simply had a spontaneous panic attack brought about by their situation, Stefan spent some time staring down at the Contract glistening on his breast. The upside-down yellow triangle looked far, far too much like the little yellow badges that the Nazis forced Jews to wear in Dachau. He wondered if that was an unhappy coinci-dence or if Ha-Satan had cheekily redesigned the

Contract, transforming a symbol of powerlessness into one of divine strength.

Stefan waited for the rest of his comrades to settle in, and then, with excitement and anxiousness bubbling in his chest, he shut his eyes and thought: *I want to go to Zone N-74.*

There was a familiar feeling, the sort of stomach-whumping exhilaration that he had experienced on roller coasters and in convertibles driven by his foolhardy boyfriend during a romantic venture out to the country. For a second, it felt like he was falling. Darkness—cold in a way that almost made it feel like icy fire—nipped at his skin.

And then he was sitting on a huge chair—more a throne than a chair, really. A throne of silver threads.

Stefan sat up and found himself in a hexagonal room. There didn't appear to be a ceiling. Instead, the grey walls stretched endlessly upwards until they vanished into a black dot. He looked down at the floor and blinked twice. The hexagonal room possessed no torches or lamps. Instead, the only source of light was a giant glowing yellow triangle that took up most of the otherwise black floor. The triangle pointed towards a short hallway that led to a single black door decorated with yet another yellow triangle.

Ah, Stefan thought. *This is the Master Room he mentioned. Satan really likes the yellow-triangle branding.*

Stefan leapt off the cushy seat and began exploring the Master Room. First, he spun around to look at the wall behind the silver throne. There were glistening crimson letters above the throne that spelled out:

HERE SITS

THE

GOD OF

ZONE N-74

Stefan glanced at one wall on the left and found a golden plaque.

THE MASTERS OF ZONE N-74

Above that, like some strange employee-of-the-month shrine, was a single portrait. A portrait of Stefan himself. He shivered as he looked at the picture that he had never posed for, at the clean, groomed, poker-faced rendition of himself. The white frame around his portrait bore a tiny plaque: **Master 1.** He was Zone N-74's first Master, then.

Stefan glanced at another wall and found that it was occupied by a large, misty mirror. He stepped forward and glanced up at the arch. The mirror's silver frame was topped by a golden carving of an eyeball. He looked at the glass but couldn't see his own reflection in the fog.

Forgetting about the mirror, Stefan turned to another corner of the hexagon. He stumbled towards a wall which boasted two clocks. One looked relatively normal save for the fact that it was decorated with golden letter spelling out, "Earth." The other clock, which was labeled "Zone," possessed two hands; the larger one pointed towards the hundred dashes around the clock's border while the smaller hand offered six options: *Day(s), Week(s), Month(s), Year(s), Centuries, Millenia.*

It took Stefan a moment to realize what the clocks were for: setting the speed of time in the Zone. He could set it so that one hour on Earth was a century in the Zone, or set the Zone one-to-one with Earth time. That could be useful. He could extend the torment that his sinful Subjects suffered for as long as he wished.

Stefan decided, for simplicity's sake, to set the Zone's time one-to-one with Earth, and then he wandered towards the final wall. On a wooden display platform there was a book that was as thick as three bibles. He only spared a brief glance at the cover. *Will to Power: A Manual for Masters. Vol. 42035.*

"Yeah, no," said Stefan, leaving the Manual to collect dust. He had never been much of a reader anyway. Stefan preferred to learn what he needed on the fly, and so, without even glancing inside the book, he started down the hall and exited the Master Room.

"What the fuck is going on here?!"

Hardly had Stefan exited the Master Room when he found himself in the midst of a burned Jewish *shtetl.* There were no Jews to be seen, however: only a small battalion of Nazis wearing bloodstained uniforms and confused expressions. Some squirmed in fear, some trembled like they'd just barely survived a car crash, and one of them, snarling with typical Nazi arrogance, marched right to up Stefan.

No time to learn like the present. Stefan recalled that Ha-Satan had told him he could override his Subject's free will with mere words and intent. He summoned his willpower right then and was surprised at the resonance his voice took on when he spoke his first Command. ***"Stop, and don't take another step."***

The Contract on Stefan's breast glowed scarlet, and before the Nazi could even think of getting within a foot of his new God, his eyes went wide with utter and complete agony as he froze in place.

"W-what…?" choked the nearly paralyzed Nazi. "It… it *hurts…*"

"Yeah?" Stefan said. He strolled right up to the frozen Nazi, pressed his finger to the child-murderer's skull, and pushed him to the ground. The Subject, still unable to move a muscle, collapsed to the dirt like the pathetic piece of trash that he was.

"Good," Stefan hissed, lifting his gaze to the other fourteen monsters. No longer the strapping, sneering superior men they had claimed to be in life, the dead Nazis huddled together like sheep, shaking in their jackboots.

Stefan smirked and cracked his knuckles. "This is going to be fun," he declared, and it was.

———— ▽ ————

Chapter
TWO

Before

The shitshow started about eleven years before Stefan found his first mass grave and became the God of Zone N-74. Eleven years, give or take. The passage of time was foggy for him sometimes. Events that lasted years had seemingly only lasted months, and events that lasted mere days seemed, in his memory, to have taken an eternity.

Stefan's earliest memory that was clear as a current event, that he could remember down to the taste in his mouth, was being sixteen, walking into his house with a cheerful smile on his face, and getting punched by his father.

"You fucking disgrace!" Herr Harkel roared, and while Stefan had been hit before—for talking in church, for telling his little brother Gerhard where babies came from, for being generally rude and obnoxious and rebellious— the corporal punishment that he had received for those minor sins had been bearable. His father would give him a little spanking or a slap on the wrist with a sigh, a roll of his eyes, and a paternal, "Don't do that again."

This hit was different. Delivered with the brutality Herr Harkel had described using during the Great War. A hit hard enough to rattle teeth and shatter jaws, a hit that sent Stefan tumbling to the floor. He heard his mother scream, not in horror but rage. He heard Arvin, the family dog, barking hysterically from the bathroom, where his parents had no doubt imprisoned the mutt lest he try to defend his favorite person.

And then he heard his little brother trot down the stairs and yelp in terror: "Stefan!"

"Gerhard, no, don't go near him!" their mother cried, grabbing the eight-year-old before he could run to his big brother. Stefan's vision had been too bleary to see his brother's face, but he would still hear those ripping sobs sometimes when he tried to sleep. Gerhard was something of a crybaby. He cried when Stefan told him that Saint Nicholas wasn't real, he cried when Stefan was too busy to play model trains with him, he cried when his glasses fogged up in the rain. This, however, was worse than his usual sobbing. It sounded like he was being murdered.

In the future, when Stefan knew what eight-year-olds sounded like when they were being murdered, he would realize that Gerhard really had made approximately the same sound.

"You *fucking faggot!*" Herr Harkel snarled, delivering a kick to Stefan's side that would still sting over a decade later. The slur spat by his father made a strange sense of resignation wash over Stefan. *Ah,* he might have thought if he weren't too full of fear to think right then, *that explains it.*

Stefan would never figure out exactly how his parents had discovered that he was a homosexual. It could have been anything, really. Maybe the grocer's son that he'd lost interest in after their third tumble had tattled on him. Maybe that nosy Frau Schmidt had seen him kiss that boy behind the church the other day.

Stefan was a reckless person by nature, and while he had been closeted at the time, it had been more out of self-interest than shame. He hadn't been suicidal back then, and so he hadn't wanted to give his father a reason to beat him to death.

But now the secret was out. Stefan's life was over. Either his father would kill him, or he'd toss him into the street and let him die of starvation.

The beating itself probably wasn't that bad—then again, maybe that was wishful thinking on his part. Wishful thinking borne from the stubborn vestiges of love he had for a father that he didn't want to believe would beat him to death for being queer. *He probably didn't beat me that hard*, that stupid little part of him would insist even though he would never receive a beating from an SS man that hurt more than the one he got from his father.

And in the same vein, maybe he had also imagined that his father's crimson face had been covered in tears. Maybe, because it would have been nice to know that Herr Harkel hated that day as much as Stefan.

However bad the beating was, it eventually ended with Stefan's mother clutching the wailing Gerhard close to her cross-clad chest and begging her husband to throw the queer out. Herr Harkel complied, grabbing the beaten boy by his throat and dragging him out the door.

"If I ever see your face again, I'll fucking kill you!" barked Herr Harkel before he threw Stefan off the porch and into a pile of snow. He slammed the door shut, and for some time, the sound of Stefan's parents shouting, Gerhard sobbing, and Arvin barking continued from inside the Harkel household. Eventually, evening turned into night and silence reigned.

The snow helped. Stefan lay face-down for a little while, every inch of his body aching, but the iciness numbed the physical pain enough that he was able to sit up. For some time, he simply stared at the door of what had once been his home, wondering what to do.

He considered staying where he was, sitting in the snow and letting what would happen happen. If he died of frostbite and his parents found him in their yard tomorrow morning, a queer icicle, fine.

And if the cold didn't kill him, maybe he could risk it. Maybe the morning would mellow out his father. Maybe Herr Harkel would be grateful to see his son. Maybe he would emerge from the house with tears in his eyes, give Stefan a hug, and say that he was sorry, that he loved his son no matter what.

Yeah, right. And maybe Hitler would convert to Judaism.

When Stefan tried to move, the pain was so intense that he almost considered staying and waiting for his father to come out and kill him. Every bone ached, every atom burned, but nevertheless, he gritted his teeth, whimpered, and stood. He was willing to accept that his life was over, but he would rather go out and die alone than stay and risk hearing his little brother cry again.

And so, with only the shirt on his back, Stefan limped away from the building that was no longer his home.

And that was how Stefan Harkel became homeless at sixteen.

▽

THE YEARS OF HOMELESSNESS WERE A BLUR OF MISERY FOR Stefan Harkel, who was, if nothing else, grateful that he could forget such long stretches of terrible time. He remembered sleeping under a lot of bridges amongst veterans and former brokers rendered homeless by the repeated economic collapses Germany suffered. He remembered getting beaten up a lot, often having his meager possessions stolen. He remembered taking a lot of odd jobs and sleeping with a lot of men that were far too old for him. He remembered that he never stayed in one place for too long.

If someone had stopped him during his wanderings and asked him what he was looking for, his first answer would have been a warm meal, his second answer would have been a decent bed, and his third answer would have been to clam up because he would have never admitted what he actually wanted. A family to replace the one that had cast him out. A family that he could truly belong to.

He thought that it would be impossible to find such a family, but then one day, he saw a recruitment poster for the *Sturmabteilung*. The SA, the paramilitary wing of the Nazi Party. Stefan asked around town, interviewed a few members, liked what they had to say, and so he signed up.

If Stefan were to think about it—which he barely had at the time, he didn't do a lot of thinking in general, it was a miracle he'd lasted so long given how little thinking he tended to do—he might have realized how odd and stupid the whole thing was. Later, much later, when the Nazi Party and killing queers became synonymous, it would be utterly baffling to an outsider.

But back then, it had made sense. Well, it hadn't made sense, but he had forced it to make sense. He was queer, yes, but he was also German. He wanted a better, stronger Germany. A Germany powerful enough that she could finally cast off her shackles. A Germany that could rescue the veterans and brokers from under her bridges.

And he didn't like communists. Fuck Marx and his weird utopian bullshit. Workers of the world unite? The workers of the world thought that Stefan Harkel was a degenerate faggot, and every time he'd come out to the workers of the world, they'd tried to beat him to death with whatever tools they'd happened to have on hand.

Workers were just like the masses: stupid, ignorant, and in desperate need of a strong hand to smack them into line. Fascism made complete sense to Stefan. The less power that stupid, ignorant people had, the better.

Stefan was also pretty sure he didn't like Jews, although he wasn't sure how many he had encountered in his short life. The problem with Jews was that it was hard to distinguish them from gentiles unless they were annoying about their Jewishness.

And anyway, even if the Nazis didn't like queers, that hardly made them special. Nobody else liked queers.

So screw it. Might as well. The uniforms looked good anyway, and the men looked even better. They didn't require him to read *Mein Kampf*, so he joined. Not because he was a homeless little waif that didn't believe a word of Hitler's speeches and just wanted to be able to eat—he was ready to laugh at all the idiots who would try to claim desperation when the war crimes trials commenced. Stefan joined the SA because he wanted to be a Nazi.

And he wasn't the only one either. The SA was home to many queer men like him; rebellious and masculine queer men eager to create a new world. A world that would reward them for their toughness. A world where masculinity was celebrated in all of its facets. A lot of them stayed in the closet, but plenty didn't. Some even proudly boasted of their orientation. The man in charge of Stefan's SA troop was one such bold queer. Wilhelm Vogel. He was all the way out of the closet, so far out of the closet that the closet was boarded shut behind him.

Wilhelm had published articles declaring that the Nazi Party should accept homosexuals openly. He argued that homosexuality was a proud and manly tradition practiced by the bold Spartans and the world-conquering Romans, a tradition that was not at all represented by the feminine little fairies that gave good queer men like him a bad name. The future of Germany, he said, should be a national *Männerbund.* Women would be little more than baby-making machines, and men could be real men.

Ernst Röhm, the homosexual head of the SA, apparently liked Vogel quite a bit. Maybe a little too much.

Wilhelm certainly wasn't Stefan's type, though that didn't matter since Wilhelm was religious about not screwing subordinates. He didn't judge Röhm for screwing him, but he said on multiple occasions that he would never forgive himself if he touched one of "his" boys. They were a gaggle of fascist little brothers to Wilhelm, and towards Stefan, the youngest in the troop, he was downright paternal. Wilhelm bought Stefan brand new clothes. He always gave him car magazines since he knew that Stefan loved vehicles of every sort. He gently chastised Stefan when he was too reckless and got himself hurt.

Wilhelm always greeted Stefan with a fatherly embrace. The first time he did that, which was also the first time Stefan put on a Nazi uniform, Stefan had been at once startled and suspicious. After some time had passed and he learned that Wilhelm didn't have any ulterior motives, Stefan accepted the hugs, on the surface only begrudgingly, in his heart with desperate gusto.

Stefan would never admit how much he looked forward to seeing Wilhelm every day so he could get a damn hug from the man. He would never mention how, for all the sex he'd had on the streets, he had always wanted to be given a platonic touch. A simple unconditional embrace. The sort that his father had once given him before he'd known what Stefan was.

In the SA, Stefan never needed to pretend to be

anything less than the rowdy, violent, cynical, fascist homosexual that he was.

Stefan missed it sometimes. The Black Foxes were nothing like Wilhelm Vogel's troop. It was a small miracle that the Black Foxes didn't personally hand every pink-triangle clad prisoner they happened upon back to the nearest SS troop with a "sorry we stole your disgusting queer" card.

Additionally, there was a rigid impersonalness to the entire Black Fox movement. The SA had been a family, brothers in arms, made up of friends and lovers who all knew each other's birthdays and bought each other gifts and gave each other hugs. Meanwhile, the Black Foxes didn't even know each other's names.

Stefan missed being a Nazi.

Sometimes.

Until they found another pit full of butchered babies. Then he would feel like a monster for missing it, and then he would flit down to Zone N-74 and set the monsters he owned on fire.

▽

Chapter
THREE

1943

I t had been four years since the war had started, but the passage of time didn't make the sight of frightened, desperate orphans any less harrowing. Stefan never got used to it. He imagined that the Subjects in his Zone—now numbering fifty-seven Nazis, the partisans had been doing good work apparently—similarly never got used to being set on fire.

Nevertheless, Stefan and his men were glad that they'd managed to save this pack of Jewish children before the Nazis had time to send them to any one of the many death camps that now marred Europe's face. The Black Foxes had ambushed a truck carrying a literal orphanage's worth of children to God-knows-where, and they'd managed to get away with only scrapes and bruises.

Trekking across the Reich with two-dozen nine-year-olds could hardly be considered easy, though frankly, even though Stefan had always hated kids, the ones he typically ended up shepherding were abominably well-behaved.

They never cried, never whined about being hungry, never asked to go to the bathroom. That was probably because they had endured four years of dehumanization. The children who asked for a bathroom break were the first to die.

An unpleasant thought, but Stefan didn't dwell on it. The kids made it as easy as they could, and so he managed to safely deliver them to two people who could handle the orphans better than he: his superior, Black Fox One, and the Black Foxes' designated child-smuggler, Black Fox 860.

"Good work," said Black Fox One when Stefan and his troop arrived at the meet-up spot in the woods. Black Fox One wore black from head to toe: black body armor, black boots, a black hood, and a black gas mask that covered her face and rendered her gender ambiguous until she spoke.

If Stefan had known more women like Black Fox One before, he might have abandoned being a misogynist sooner. Black Fox One was, simply put, a tough bitch. A great fighter, a great shooter, and great at coming up with curse-laden insults for anyone she didn't like. Stefan wished they were allowed to talk about themselves in the Black Foxes because he would have loved to know how Black Fox One became the way she was.

Stefan nodded brusquely and then glanced at the short, unmasked man standing beside Black Fox One. Eight-Sixty was scrawny and small and everything Stefan loathed in fellow queer. (And he was a queer, Stefan could sense it. Frustration and an urge to screw something had even led Stefan to proposition him at one point only for Eight-Sixty to smile, blush, and announce that he was flattered but taken. Prude.)

However, physically weak and obnoxiously feminine as he was, Eight-Sixty was also really damn nice. An absolute mother goose of a human being. If he were a woman, he'd be wearing a giant, puffy dress just so orphans could huddle under it. He loved kids, and he was good with them, somehow possessing the ability to make them smile even when their parents were dead and they'd witnessed horrors that would never leave their nightmares.

And that was something none of the other Black Foxes could do, make those poor kids smile. So even if he was weak, Eight-Sixty was valuable. And for that reason, Stefan decided that it would be best if his men went with Eight-Sixty to deliver the children to their next safehouse.

"You sure, Five?" Black Fox One said when he announced as much. "If you want to wait here, I can probably go get Black Fox Two and he could..."

Stefan grunted. No. *No.* He would *not* rely on Black Fox One's crazy boyfriend. Maybe the other Black Foxes could forget, forgive, move on, but not Stefan. Never.

"He has more important things to do than chaperone me, One," Stefan said, jabbing his thumb towards the six men trailing him. "Besides, I could use a break from these idiots. I'll start heading towards Base Twelve. Check the radio, see if Papa Fox has anything else for me, start restocking maybe."

Stefan had never actually met Papa Fox, the illustrious and mysterious leader of the Black Foxes, face-to-face. Few people had, even in the top ranks of the Black Foxes. The people of Europe knew Papa Fox by his voice alone, which they heard via the secret Black Fox Radio Station that Papa Fox maintained to spread anti-Nazi messages to the masses and secret codes to his agents.

Stefan didn't know what Papa Fox looked like, but he did know one thing about his leader that few people did: Papa Fox was a Master.

Stefan only knew that because of a single encounter he'd had with Papa Fox's technician, one of his chief lieutenants, Rabbi Gedaliah. Gedaliah had been one of the men who had helped form the Black Foxes. During the early days of the movement, he and Stefan had talked often. After the war started, they only saw each other once, and both had been surprised to see a telltale yellow triangle on one another's breasts. Apparently, only other Masters could see signed Contracts.

Gedaliah and Stefan hadn't been able to chat for very long, and the Rabbi, who was Master of Zone N-6, hadn't been particularly impressed by Stefan's low-level Contract to Zone N-74. Nevertheless, the Rabbi had mentioned before he'd been forced to rush off that Papa Fox himself was also a Master, more specifically Ernst Röhm's Master. That had made sense: it explained how Papa Fox knew exactly what to say on Black Fox Radio, exactly how to press Hitler and Heydrich's buttons.

On occasion, Stefan felt bad for his old boss, but not very bad. Röhm had always been a creep anyway. At least in Hell, he could be put to good use.

"Sa—err, One-Twenty! There you are!"

Black Fox 120, the youngest man in Stefan's troop, had been taking a leak behind a tree and was forced to run in order to catch up with the pack. One-Twenty offered a small smile to Eight-Sixty and embraced him in that platonic way that heterosexual men who weren't constantly worried about sending the wrong message did.

Another reason to like Eight-Sixty: he was One-Twenty's closest friend, and the Russian Black Fox with the brilliant blue eyes needed a friend after what he had been through.

That was a bad memory. One of the worst, actually, which was saying quite a bit since Stefan's life occasionally felt like nothing more than a parade of bad memories. He and his men (and two women, but he wasn't sure what to call a mixed army, so "men" would do) had been following the German forces after Hitler's invasion of the Soviet

Union. More specifically, they'd been tracking the Beast of Belorussia, *Einsatzgruppen* commander Viktor Naden, an ugly monster who apparently got a kick out of burning Jews alive.

Stefan had been hoping to kill the shithead and then, Satan willing, receive a pleasant surprise in the form of Viktor Naden's name appearing on his Contract. Unfortunately, Naden was a slippery snake and had always managed to stay one destroyed village ahead of them.

Naden rarely left survivors, but in the village of Khruvina, he left one. Stefan had found the teenager just outside the ruins of Khruvina's scorched synagogue with a bullet wound above his heart. He'd nursed the teen back to health, and the sole survivor had all but demanded to be allowed into the Black Foxes, declaring with a fiery gleam in his eyes that he was going to make Viktor Naden *pay*.

Far be it from Stefan to stop someone from killing Nazis, and besides, he had recognized the desperate fury in the teen's eyes. He knew that if he said no, the boy would just go after Naden by himself and probably get killed. And so Stefan had welcomed the boy from Khruvina into the Black Foxes.

Stefan liked the Russian boy, Black Fox 120, more than he liked any other Black Fox. Maybe because he sort of reminded Stefan of himself, particularly during those foolhardy early days when One-Twenty would constantly abandon his posts and assignments if he got even a whiff of Viktor Naden's scent. That recklessness was as charming as it was annoying, though Stefan had also been pained by the desperateness of it. The sorrow and rage that drove One-Twenty was understandable and tragic, and Stefan hoped that torturing Viktor Naden to death would soothe the Russian's spirit.

But then...well, shit, Stefan frankly didn't know what

had happened. One day, after abandoning his post to chase Naden again, One-Twenty had vanished. Stefan had written the Russian off for dead with not a small bit of hand-wringing. But then, One-Twenty had rematerialized with a new friend in the form of the man who would become Eight-Sixty.

After that, One-Twenty was different. Still a good fighter, still determined to kill Nazis, but he wasn't sullen. He actually smiled sometimes. Viktor Naden was eventually sent to the Eastern Front, and was presumably killed in action, hopefully slowly and painfully, but One-Twenty never even mentioned his name again.

Stefan was glad. Vengeance was all well and good, but Viktor Naden had been One-Twenty's chain, and now he was free of him in more ways than one. Stefan didn't know exactly how that liberation had come about, but he had a feeling that Eight-Sixty's friendship had something to do with it.

Eight-Sixty and One-Twenty exchanged a bit of banter and a few anecdotes about what they'd been doing on their separate assignments before Eight-Sixty turned his attention to the children, who crowded around him. Stefan indulged for a moment, watching sullen faces brighten as Eight-Sixty knelt before them and offered a friendly smile and calm reassurances. Black Fox One cleared her throat.

"All right. We can meet up at the Bunker if you want," she said. "But take at least one of your men along with you. Don't go *completely* alone."

"I'll go with him!" a Russian accented voice piped up, and Stefan snorted.

"Eavesdropper," he accused as One-Twenty stepped forward. "You know, in some armies, you get executed for listening in on your superiors."

"Shoot me, then," said One-Twenty. Stefan couldn't

see Black Fox One's face since it was hidden by her gas mask, but he could *feel* her rolling her eyes.

"Don't tempt me. I wanna shoot all of you boys sometimes," she said. "All right, One-Twenty, you stay with Five. Eight-Sixty and the rest are with me."

"Got it. Can I pinch some ammo off'a ya?" Stefan said, checking his gun. "We bumped into some SS shitheads on the way here."

"Not a problem," One said, shoving a clip of bullets into his arms. "Hope you sent 'em to Hell."

Stefan cackled and glanced down at the Contract glowing above his heart. "Oh, don't worry. We did."

Chapter
FOUR

For a very long time, Stefan operated under the assumption that he was not going to fall in love.

When he was very young and very stupid, before he joined the SA and somehow got even stupider, he had actually thought that it was impossible for queers to fall in love. Of course, he knew the details of his parents' dead marriage well enough that he had also doubted whether or not heterosexuals *actually* fell in love. Maybe the whole notion of love was just a mass delusion. A conspiracy.

Of course, Stefan also hadn't particularly *wanted* to fall in love. He was impulsive and liked to have fun, and that suited him fine. The notion of finding a nice boy and, what, pretending they were just roommates for the rest of their lives? Didn't appeal to him at all. Dates, nice restaurants, a romantic night in a hotel room? Give him a good-looking man in an alleyway or a park or a locker room, that was all he needed.

Besides, Stefan saw how the other men in the SA were about their boyfriends, and it was absolutely disgusting. "Oh, I think he was looking at Peter the other day, and he promised we'd meet after that speech but then he…" *Bla bla bla.* If he ever wasted a second of his few years of existence sitting with his cheek in his hand and sighing because of a man, he'd eat a bullet.

Love, it seemed, made men into weak little waifs. Stefan wasn't about to seek out such a terrible fate. He was perfectly happy flitting from man to man, enjoying his time without anything tying him down.

And then he met Axel Lahner.

Their relationship started when Axel slapped his ass. Certainly not the most romantic gesture, but it got the idea across, and Stefan had never been one for daintily waltzing around a man he fancied.

Stefan certainly hadn't been subtle about the fact that he found his fellow Stormtrooper dashing. He had been giving Lahner bedroom eyes at every beer hall brawl, speech, and march they attended since the day Axel had joined Vogel's little family.

Stefan could hardly help himself: Axel Lahner was hands-down, no-contest the most gorgeous man that he had ever seen. The very definition of tall, dark, and handsome. Six feet tall with onyx black hair always perfectly combed to the side, strikingly beautiful silver eyes, and a smile worthy of a fairy-tale prince.

He was the sort of man that brought about feelings of horny jealousy in Stefan. Stefan was neither drop-dead ugly nor drop-dead gorgeous: average height, average messy brown hair, average brown eyes, average everything. If he hadn't been relatively confident, he might have figured that he didn't have a snowball's chance in Hell of getting to screw Axel Lahner even once.

For some time, though, Stefan thought that Axel might

have been the rare heterosexual man in Vogel's Troop since he didn't see the man flirt with any of his comrades. Stefan all but gave up, resigned to the fact that women got all the best men, until one little incident made him realize that Axel was not heterosexual. Rather, he was simply very good at hiding himself, a talent that typically wasn't necessary in Vogel's Troop, but which Lahner seemed determined to maintain, nonetheless.

Axel got across his real intentions one day when Stefan happened to bend down to get something out of a duffel bag. When he did so, he felt a slap right on his ass. Not a flirtatiously gentle slap, no, a slap that made Stefan leap up and grab his bottom, letting out a very unattractive yelp of pain. Every Brownshirt in the room laughed at him.

Stefan whirled around and scowled at the guilty party only to find that Axel wasn't laughing. Smirking, yes. Smirking a devilishly familiar smirk. Axel took advantage of the fact that all of their comrades were blinded by tears of laughter and shot Stefan a wink, nudging his head in the vague direction of a hallway with a broom closet.

Stefan's anger immediately turned into burning excitement. It was actually a struggle to wait until his comrades had quieted down, wait until the larger conversation returned to the depravity of Jewry, wait until Axel stepped out "for a smoke," and then wait even more, until he could stand it no more and followed Lahner.

He found Axel leaning against a wall by the very familiar broom closet, fiddling impatiently with an unlit cigarette. When Stefan approached, Axel glanced here and there, silver eyes flashing with the cautiousness of a mouse bracing itself to venture out of his hole to get a very sumptuous piece of cheese.

When Axel decided that the coast was clear, his silver eyes fell upon Stefan and glistened eagerly. He shoved the cigarette back into his pocket and smiled that princely smile of his. "Ah, Harkel. Sorry about that. I didn't intend on hurting you, but you know, you can't just leave yourself unguarded like that in…"

"Yeah, yeah," Stefan said impatiently, grabbing Axel by his black tie, pushing and pulling at once: pulling him into a kiss and pushing him through the broom closet door.

The closet was dark, but Stefan was so familiar with it by now that he could have been blind and still easily maneuvered his beau into the best, cleanest corner. Axel didn't fight or whimper when Stefan deepened the kiss, and in fact he kissed back quite enthusiastically, but Stefan could nevertheless feel him trembling.

"Y-you're…" Axel gasped when they finally broke apart.

"Forward?" Stefan supplied.

"Impatient," Axel said, and even in the scant light of the closet, Stefan could see that the other man's face was positively crimson. It was adorable, really. Stefan was almost tempted to pinch his cheek, but instead he focused on unbuttoning Axel's uniform.

"Sorry, Lahner, next time I'll bring champagne," Stefan quipped, kissing him once more, deep and eager, utterly convinced that they probably wouldn't screw again.

"Wait," Axel grunted when Stefan started to undo his belt. "Wait, stop…"

And Stefan did, because he might have been an asshole, but he was not a complete and utter piece of shit. He started to pull away, ready to shrug and assure Axel that there were no hard feelings even though he couldn't pretend that he wasn't disappointed. Before he could even fully let Lahner go, however, his comrade grabbed his arms.

"Sorry, I think there was a misunderstanding," Axel

said, offering a charming, frisky smile. "I don't…err… well, *you know*…"

Oh. This was going to be fun.

In one swift motion, he pinned Axel against the wall again, now pressing their bodies against one another. Axel let out a yelp of surprise that became a whimper of pleasure.

"There's been a misunderstanding all right," Stefan purred. "You seem to think that you're *in charge.*"

"I…I…I…*ah!*" Whatever Axel was about to say, he was cut off when Stefan unbuckled his pants. Stefan, of course, would have stopped if Axel told him to, but it was abundantly clear that Axel didn't want him to.

"You wanna keep going, Lahner?"

"Y-yes!"

"Yes, what?"

"Y-Yes, sir!"

———————— ▽ ————————

THE DAY AFTER STEFAN AND AXEL HAD THEIR FUN IN THE broom closet, Axel nearly got his head blown off.

It started with a brawl, a brawl that Wilhelm and his Brownshirts provoked when they kicked down the door to a communist hideout. The Reds had been having some kind of meeting. Wilhelm had claimed that they were plotting against the Nazis, but frankly, they could have been holding a Soviet book club for all Stefan cared. He liked to fight, liked to crack skulls. It made him feel manly, and it made him feel like he had some control in the world, and also *fuck communists.*

The brawl went like it usually did; Stefan knocked out some teeth, though this time he found himself focusing less on how much he was hurting his opponent and more on how Axel was hurting *his* opponent. Unlike Stefan, whose fighting style was thoughtless and brutal, Axel moved with royal grace, dodging Bolshevik blows, defeating his opponent with one well-delivered strike to the face or spine. Damn him. Good looking, tall, great at sex, an amazing fighter. Stefan wondered if there was anything Axel *wasn't* good at.

His answer came right as he knocked down his opponent and looked up: Axel wasn't good at sensing when there was a gun aimed at his head.

"Watch it!" Stefan cried, diving across a table and knocking Axel to the ground as one communist aimed a pistol at the taller SA man. Smoke filled the small space, and Stefan felt the bullet whizz right over his ear before he and Axel tumbled to the ground together.

"Fucking Jew!" Stefan heard Wilhelm shout as he tackled the Bolshevik. "I've got his gun!"

That made Stefan breathe a sigh of relief, and as the adrenaline died down, he realized that he was practically straddling Axel. He looked down at his comrade, whose face was as red as the man who had almost shot him.

"Hi," Stefan said in an attempt to alleviate the sexual tension. It didn't work.

"T-Thanks," Axel stuttered. He was far, far too cute right then, and so Stefan took advantage of the smoke. He leaned down and gave his comrade a quick but harsh kiss before jumping off him.

"Need a hand?" Stefan said, offering his. Axel took it silently, trembling and blushing and looking absolutely terrified.

"Nice save there, Stefan!" cackled Wilhelm, shoving the communist's gun into his bag. The other Brownshirts swiftly looted the place, and once they were through, Wilhelm commanded everyone to head home quickly before the cops showed.

"Hey, wait," Axel said before Stefan could run after

the other Nazis who lived in the barracks with Wilhelm. Axel grabbed his savior's hand, and while Stefan usually preferred not to sleep with the same man twice, the jolt of excitement that went through his body made him decide immediately that he would make an exception. He turned and readied himself to suggest a decent alleyway far from the den of now-unconscious communists, but Axel, having seemingly gotten his bearings, flashed a rather soft smile.

"Come back to my apartment with me," Axel said.

"Apartment?" Stefan repeated uncertainly. He had noticed that Axel was one of the very few people in Vogel's Troop who didn't live in the barracks. A single man couldn't afford a private space in such harsh economic times, after all. The fact that Axel had an apartment meant that he needed privacy, and if he needed privacy, that meant he likely had a wife and children.

That in and of itself wouldn't have been the biggest issue for Stefan, who didn't care very much about other people's unhappy marriages. He didn't often follow men back to their home, but on the rare occasions he had, his need for some form of exciting danger had been fulfilled by the fact that his lover's ignorant wife could come home at any moment.

He had stopped screwing married men some time ago, however. Not out of any moral qualms, but because the sex was always terrible, and he was sick of his partners rushing him out of the house like he was some sort of plague-infested rat after they'd quenched their thirst.

Axel must have seen Stefan's hesitancy, because he tightened his grip on the shorter man's hand and smiled reassuringly. "We'll have privacy. It's *my* apartment, only mine. Well…"

Axel chuckled and raked a hand through his dark hair. "I suppose it's technically my father's apartment since he pays for it."

"Papa's money?" Stefan quipped, and Axel laughed and nodded.

"My father's Paul Lahner," he said, like that was supposed to explain it. When Stefan gave him a shrug in response, Axel looked at once surprised and strangely delighted.

"You haven't heard of him? He's a philanthropist. Realtor. Landowner. He gives a lot of money to the National Socialist Party. Something of a well-known benefactor."

"He pays for my meals?"

Axel laughed. "Probably!"

Axel really was a prince, then. "I'll have to send him a thank-you card," Stefan said. "Your old man won't mind if we use his apartment?"

"I'm sure he'd *mind*, but he won't *know*," Axel replied, his grip slackening a bit, as though being reminded of his father's own homophobia was making him reconsider his offer. "He doesn't even live in the city."

If it were any other man, Stefan probably would have outright refused on the grounds that having sex in a safe apartment was *boring*. But this was Axel Lahner propositioning him, and he did enjoy the idea of seeing Axel naked.

"Lead the way, your majesty," said Stefan, and the walk to Axel's apartment was far, far too long because the smile that Axel gave in response lit an inferno inside him.

Once they actually reached the little apartment (which Axel assured him had very thick walls), Axel casually ushered him inside as though he was a welcome guest. That was pleasant: Stefan was too used to being shoved through doorways with anxious terror. It was nice that Axel actually held the door open for him and smiled that princely smile as he said, "After you."

Of course (and happily), the facade ended as soon as

Axel shut the door behind his guest. Stefan barely got a chance to glance around the little home because Axel suddenly lunged at him, pinning him against a wall and kissing him deeply.

"Hm?" hummed Stefan with a smile, gripping Axel's shoulders and smirking against his lips. "Someone's *forward.*"

"*Impatient,*" purred Axel, all but slamming Stefan against the wall when the slightly shorter man attempted to push him back. "If you want to be in charge, Harkel, *take charge.*"

Oh. That was new. Axel had clearly enjoyed doing things Stefan's way in the closet. Maybe he was merely trying to salvage his self-image, but from the eagerness of his tone, it was just as likely that Lahner simply wanted a challenge.

Stefan did love a challenge.

Axel struggled admirably. Stefan got well acquainted with Lahner's apartment as he and his comrade all but wrestled their way across it, stripping off their clothes all the way. It was…well, it was great.

Inevitably, Stefan won, however, and they ended up in Axel's bed, with Stefan on top. Stefan could only hope that the walls were thick, because Axel's gasps and cries of pleasure were *loud.* Not that he was complaining, of course. It was *thrilling.*

They both finished after a few minutes, and when they did, there was that moment of breathless post-coital speechlessness which, for Stefan, was typically awkward and frantic, but right then was strangely pleasant. Perhaps because Axel stared at him with a gleam in those silver eyes as he fought to catch his breath.

"Damn," Axel sighed when he finally *did* catch his breath, reaching up and brushing a hand through Stefan's sweat-soaked hair. "You're gorgeous."

And that made Stefan's steadily cooling face burn once more because he had never received a compliment *after* sex. Before sex, sure, plenty of men would tell Stefan whatever he wanted to hear if it meant getting in his pants. After they'd already gotten what they wanted, though? Never. There was no need, after all.

Which, of course, meant that Axel actually meant that. That was…Stefan wasn't entirely sure how to react to that except to say, "You too," like an idiot.

Axel laughed, and Stefan rolled off him. "Shower?" Axel offered.

"You first."

"Care to join me?" Axel offered in a teasingly flirtatious way that meant he wasn't serious but felt an obligation to offer.

"You've never screwed in the shower, have you?" snorted Stefan, and a boyish little blush bloomed on Axel's cheeks.

"Ah, hm…well, no. Is it bad?"

"Last time I tried it, I slipped and nearly cracked my skull open, so I'd file it under 'bad.'"

"Noted. Sounds like if you wanna shower at the same time, though, you just have to step outside."

Axel gestured towards the covered window, and indeed, the sound of heavy raindrops battering the blind-covered glass made it abundantly clear that it was storming heavily.

"Say, don't run off," Axel said, reaching out and grabbing Stefan's hand, lighting another spark in his gut. "Stay the night."

And once more, Stefan found himself ruffled and uncertain. He had hoped that since Axel lived by himself, he wouldn't rudely rush him out of the house, but he hadn't expected that the handsome fellow would invite him to stay the night. This was becoming less of a tryst and more of a *date.*

"You can have the bed. I'll sleep on the couch," Axel said almost hastily when he saw the hesitant look on Stefan's face. "No need for snuggling."

Stefan actually wasn't entirely sure whether he would love or hate to *snuggle.* Whatever. It was more out of curiosity and laziness that he agreed.

Axel showered swiftly and gave Stefan his turn. Stefan tried to use a minimal amount of Axel's fancy soaps, and emerged to find his clothes neatly folded on the bed. He dressed, exited the bedroom, and found Axel, groomed and pressed, standing in front of the stove with an anxious look on his face.

"Ah! I'm not a good cook," Axel said by way of apology, gesturing to the burned carrots before him, and that fetched a chuckle from Stefan.

"Not precisely a *hausfrau.* Shame," Stefan said, plopping down at the table and trying to subdue his nervous squirming. This really was entirely new territory: he rarely spared time to share a drink with a man before they screwed, much less a meal afterwards.

"Sorry. I'm used to having a cook in-house." sighed Axel, dumping his pitiful attempt at a home-cooked meal in the trash and grabbing a bottle of wine. "Well…ah…if you're hungry…"

"Drink is fine, I ate earlier. I, uhm…" Stefan nearly choked on his own tongue. "I do appreciate the thought. You don't have to do shit like that."

"No? I'm good enough that I don't have to impress you?" chuckled Axel, pouring Stefan a glass of some fancy-ass wine that was probably older than his great-grandparents. It tasted awful, but at the risk of seeming completely low-class, Stefan forced himself to down a few sips.

"There are other ways to impress me," Stefan said as Axel sat across from him.

"Oh!" Axel chuckled. "Do tell."

"Nah ah," replied Stefan, shaking his head. "You don't get any hints."

"Ah, a man of mystery, then. This seems unfair; you already know about me."

"Just that you're rich."

"Son of a rich man. I don't have a coin of my own."

Stefan chuckled. "Least you're honest. One time, a guy tried to impress me with a fancy watch he was wearing. Turned out he stole it from his grandpa."

Axel snorted, nearly spitting out his drink. "That's embarrassing."

"I mean, honestly, I'm not sure why he even bothered since I'd already agreed to screw him."

"Did you?"

Stefan nodded.

"*After* he pulled that?" Axel chortled.

"I have low standards."

"Well, now I feel bad."

"Awww, sorry, your majesty, didn't mean to hurt your feelings."

"Is 'your majesty' my name now?" Axel queried with a fond little chuckle, leaning his hand on his cheek. Stefan was struck by the fact that he'd seen couples like this before, albeit out in public: a bottle of wine, a cheek in the hand. If Axel tried to turn on the damn gramophone and slow-dance, Stefan would jump out the window, rain be damned.

"Be grateful. I could come up with a worse nickname if I wanted," Stefan said. Axel laughed again, and damn him to Hell, even his laugh was perfect.

"I'll count my blessings," Axel said, his silver eyes twinkling devilishly. "And come up with a nice nickname for you."

"Don't you dare."

"*Schnuckiputzi.*"

"I will throw this wine in your fucking face."

Axel let out a sound that was half laugh, half groan, and rubbed a hand across his face. "That's what my little brother calls my sister-in-law."

"Yuck."

"That's what I say every time I see them; they are *disgusting* together. It's like watching two birds vomit into each other's mouths."

Stefan, who rarely had much to laugh about, almost fell off his chair laughing at that visual. "I feel sorry for you!" he gasped when he finally regained the ability to speak. "Take a crowbar with you next time you go home."

"I'm tempted. Luckily, they just got married, so they're on their honeymoon right now and I won't have to worry about them for Christmas."

"Hoping they'll never come back?"

"Just a little. Of course, then my mama would only put more pressure on me to find a pretty girl, and she's already been laying it on thick since my brother got married."

Axel's genuine, dashingly handsome smile became twisted at the edges. He looked into the scarlet liquid in his cup and unleashed a heavy sigh. "I'm probably gonna have to get married myself soon. Get my own little lavender marriage."

Lavender marriage. A pretty term for what was, to Stefan, the height of ugliness: when a man, out of selfishness or cowardice or fear or resignation, stayed firmly in the closet and married a woman.

It was cruel and awful for all parties: for the man imprisoned in his own house, the woman tied to a man who would never love her, the children who would no doubt be damaged by their parents' inevitably loveless marriage. Society was cruel beyond measure for making lavender marriages exist, for making some men (*some cowards*, Stefan would think when he was being particularly uncharitable) think that it was a necessary evil.

The fact that the world thought a lavender marriage was better than someone simply remaining a "confirmed bachelor" (Stefan hated that term) was, to him, utter proof that God was either a sadist or, more likely, didn't exist.

(So much for that, Stefan would think later, when he held a piece of God's power in his hands, when he *was* a God. *Sadist it is, then.)*

"Just do what you want," Stefan said, immediately regretting his blunt stupidity. He might as well have told an injured veteran plagued by trauma to just *feel better.*

Despite his guest's insensitivity, however, Axel chuckled. "Well...if only it were that easy," he said, downing some of his wine. "Maybe it won't be too bad. There are plenty of women I like."

"You swing both ways?" Stefan said, trying and failing to mask the disdain in his voice. It was probably horribly hypocritical of him to be as biphobic as he was, but back when he had still been willing to sleep with bisexual men, he had too often heard the phrase, "I love my wife, I'm *just curious.*" Stefan didn't have many qualms about giving a man trapped in a lavender marriage a good time, but he hated being a *curiosity*, something to use and discard without the slightest bit of pain.

"Oh, no, not like that!" Axel chuckled, somewhat bitterly. "I mean that I have lots of friends who are women, so it wouldn't be as terrible for me. Some men I know can't even stand being in the same room as a woman."

Stefan raised his hand, proudly declaring, "I hate women."

"Truly?" Axel sounded at once amused and disappointed, as though he would have expected better of Stefan.

"Pretty sure most heterosexual men hate women too; they just *have* to deal with them," Stefan said, making sure that his tone was jesting even though he wasn't.

"I'm the opposite, actually," mused Axel. "For friendship, I like women far more than men."

"Are you serious?"

"Maybe because I have sisters, I don't know. I've just always gotten along better with women than I have with men in platonic settings. Almost every woman I know is very, very sweet."

Stefan most certainly didn't have the same experience; every woman that he had ever been forced to interact with had alternatively been holier-than-thou or catty to the point of absurdity. He preferred masculine bluntness to the smirking disdain women tended to give him.

"Introduce me to your female friends and maybe I'll change my mind," Stefan said with a shrug, and Axel laughed.

"I don't think I will, actually. I'd be too jealous."

"You don't have to worry about that. I'm never getting into a lavender marriage."

"Hm…you're braver than me, then. Well! Anyway! This is a heavy subject! Let's talk about something nicer! How about politics?"

Stefan feigned like he was about to toss the wine into Axel's face, but since they were both of the same political persuasion, they managed to carry on a friendly conversation about Hitler, communism, and the future of the SA.

It was…nice. Stefan wasn't usually very chatty, but there was something pleasant about talking to someone like-minded, listening to Axel offer that lovely laugh at his sarcastic quips. Before Stefan knew it, it was late into the night and his throat was sore from talking and laughing for hours.

"Damn, look at the time!" Axel chuckled. "Don't let me keep you up with my jabbering."

"I like your jabbering," confessed Stefan, doing his best to make that declaration sound casual. "But I *am* gonna go to sleep. Too much of a good thing and all that."

"You don't really seem like the sort to engage in *moderation*," teased Axel, but nonetheless, he flung himself onto his couch, offering his guest a smile and a small salute. "Good night, Harkel."

"Good night."

Stefan didn't fall asleep in Axel's bed right away— partially because Axel's sheets smelled like cigarettes, and partially because he was certain that Axel or maybe some sort of kidnapping gang would burst through the door and do something awful to him in his helpless state. Because Stefan Harkel didn't have nights this good.

But nothing happened, and eventually, he fell into a pleasant sleep.

—————— ▽ ——————

Stefan made a lot of excuses after that.

When he kept going back to Axel's apartment, he said to himself: *Well, it's fun. Best sex ever. Why wouldn't I keep going back?*

When he always ended up staying after they were done, chatting with Axel over wine and a poorly made meal, he said to himself: *Whatever, I'm hungry, and it's free food, and it'd be rude to run off when he worked hard to make it even though he's an awful cook.*

When he stopped actively seeking out other men, he said to himself: *Why would I bother when I could screw Axel instead? Waste of energy when I know we'll have better sex tonight.*

After weeks of this, as Axel was setting himself up on the couch once more, Stefan grabbed his comrade's pillow and said, "Hey, don't. Use your own damn bed. I don't care."

When he said that fully knowing that *snuggles* might follow, Stefan did so with the mental excuse that *it's his damn bed anyway, and he's hardly used it for weeks.* It wasn't as though Stefan wasn't used to sleeping way too close to men uglier than Axel. The streets full of smelly vagrants had been far less private and cozy than Axel's queen-size bed.

And besides, the look that Axel gave him would be well worth it even if Axel snored.

Axel did not snore. He did toss and turn quite a bit, but Stefan had grown up sleeping with a dog in his bed that constantly had chasing dreams, so that didn't bother him.

They didn't end up snuggling, though once in a while after they were done having sex and after Axel had finished having a smoke (his own vice, which Stefan indulged because *it's his house and he can smoke if he wants*), they did sometimes lie side-by-side, with Stefan somewhat awkwardly lying on top of Axel's arm. A half-hug, not quite a snuggle, but it did feel…good.

And for months, that was how Stefan spent most of his week: in Axel's room, sleeping not quite in his arms but on his arm.

He would have once thought that sleeping with only one man in a quiet, private little apartment would be the height of boredom, but it was oddly engaging, especially since he and Axel were able to talk well into the night. Usually about random shit: politics, dogs, Stefan and Axel's mutual hatred of children, and more often than not, cars. (One good thing about being queer: it was relatively easy for Stefan to find someone that he could have sex with who also wanted to talk about cars.)

"Fords are fucking trash," Axel said with a chuckle one night after an extensive but polite argument about the merits of the American automaker's craft. "I don't care that Henry knows about the Jewish Question."

"I like American cars," replied Stefan with a shrug, earning a snort from Axel.

"You have shitty tastes, then."

"In cars and in men."

"Ouch!" laughed Axel. "I'm wounded! If you could drive any car, what would it be?"

"Silver Ghost."

"Really?"

"The '21. Only ever seen it in magazines. Someone I knew used to work parking cars and got to park one once. He said it was *so smooth*."

"I think it would suit you. It *is* a very pretty car."

"You're calling me pretty?"

"I am, actually."

"I am not *pretty*, I am *handsome*."

"All right, the car is *handsome* then, and so it suits you since you are very *handsome*."

"Good boy." Stefan patted Axel's cheek, screwed him one more time, and then thought nothing of that conversation afterwards.

But a few days later, when he and a few boys from Wilhelm's barracks were loitering around outside breaking bottles, Stefan was nearly deafened by the beeping of a car horn. He turned to find himself facing his dream car: a dazzling silver convertible operated by a dazzling silver-eyed man.

"What the Hell?!" Stefan cried, running to the driver's side, and planting a kiss on Axel's cheek despite his lover's anxious refusal to leave the closet. Axel, comforted by the fact that nobody had seen that display of affection, smiled at Stefan.

"You like?" Axel asked, and Stefan all but swooned as he ran his hands along the vehicle.

"Of course I fucking like it, but you didn't need to buy a car to impress me!"

"I needed a car anyway. Thanks for the recommendation. Wanna take it for a spin?"

That made an embarrassed flush creep onto Stefan's face because despite his love of cars, he didn't actually know how to drive. Well, he knew *how* to drive, but he had only ever driven a car once, and that had been during an attempted vehicular theft he'd committed when he was homeless. And *that* had ended in him hitting a lamppost when he'd tried to back up.

When he told Axel all of that, his lover's eyes glistened. "Hop in, then," Axel said, patting the leather seat beside him. "I know this beautiful spot outside the city. We can enjoy the great outdoors, and you can drive without having to worry about hitting anything. Or, well, any*one.*"

"Never thought the great outdoors were that great," Stefan confessed, nonetheless leaping into the passenger's seat and grinning like a giddy toddler as he stroked the leather.

"Too many bugs?" Axel assumed.

"Too lonely." The words had barely left Stefan's lips when he regretted them. He hadn't intended to sound so needy. Axel, however, only chuckled fondly.

"Well, you won't be lonely this time!" he said, revving up the engine. "Let's see if I can get you to appreciate nature."

They zoomed out of the city limits, past the poster-covered streets and synagogue full of Orthodox Jews that Stefan, Axel, and the rest of Wilhelm's Troop occasionally tormented, past the woods. It was a rush just to be a passenger, sticking his head out of the side of the car like a dog and letting the wind whip at his face, listening to Axel teasingly declare that Stefan was lucky he was handsome despite what the wind would do to his hair.

At last, they found themselves in a great stretch of green guarded by a few mountains, dotted with only a few trees and cut in half by a brook. The road here was long and lonely. Civilization and all its prying eyes were miles and miles away.

"Switch!" Axel declared, and Stefan did so eagerly. Perhaps unsurprisingly, he was as reckless behind the wheel as he was in every other capacity. He laughed as he tested the limits of the machine, driving to and fro, circling the few trees and enjoying the hoots from Axel that were at once carefree and terrified.

"You're crazy!" Axel yelped, and Stefan was barely able to hear that fond declaration above the whipping of the wind and the irate squawking of birds disturbed by the roaring of the engine.

Finally, and perhaps inevitably, a bug flew right into Stefan's eye, and he was forced to bring the car to a halt.

"Owww, owww," Stefan laughed, unable to stop smiling even as his eye burned. He did his best to blink the bug out of his cornea while Axel cackled at his misery.

"That bug sacrificed his life to save the world from your driving," Axel joked, fighting to catch his breath before he leaned back and fished a cigarette and a lighter out of his pocket.

"Try?" Axel offered once Stefan had dislodged the bug from his eye, and Stefan shook his head.

"Hitler hates those, you know," Stefan said. Stefan hated them too, though probably not for whatever brilliant reason Hitler did. He had memories—once fond, now bitter—of his father smoking. He remembered when his father had let him try one of his cigarettes for his twelfth birthday. He remembered coughing horribly while his father laughed and patted him on the back. *The cough means it's working,* he'd said, because he insisted that smoking cleaned the lungs of dust and debris and added years to one's life.

Herr Harkel had probably made that up to convince Stefan's mother that the smokey smell that clung to every inch of the Harkel household was warranted. That, or he believed every propaganda piece the cigarette companies put out.

Axel smirked, inhaled deeply, and blew a puff of smoke into the perfectly clean mountain air. "Hitler isn't here," he said, and then he reached over and grabbed Stefan's thigh, squeezing it and purring, *"Nobody's* here."

Stefan's reaction was immediate. His smile became a look of pure severity, and he shoved Axel's hand off of him. "No."

"What?" Axel sounded both disappointed and surprised. Stefan pointed to the greenery outside.

"We're *not* fucking in this beautiful car, asshole," he said. "We are *not* messing it up. Out."

"I…"

"Out."

"Y-yes, sir."

Stefan had screwed men in parks before, which was usually one of his least favorite places for sex simply because grass tickled, and he hated to be interrupted because he became convinced that there was a big-ass bug crawling up his leg.

It was different out here, in the bright light of day, isolated with Axel. Cleaner, less bugs, plenty of space, and they could both be as loud as they liked. And they were loud.

They kissed much longer than they were usually wont

to once they were done, because Axel didn't break away and Stefan didn't really want him to. When they finally separated, it was with a laugh.

"I'll get your clothes," Axel offered, rushing over to the small pile he and Stefan had left by the beautiful, still-unsullied silver car.

"Thanks, your majesty," chuckled Stefan, standing and catching his clothes as Axel tossed them at him.

"Well, Lahner," mused Stefan as he pulled up his pants and fumbled with his shirt. "I'll give you credit; you made me enjoy nature."

"Axel."

The firmly gentle request echoed in Stefan's ears for a moment, and he hesitated to poke his head out of his shirt because he knew that once he did, he would behold those glistening silver eyes and wouldn't be able to refuse what-ever Axel asked for. He inhaled deeply, thrust his head out of the hole, and found that Axel, still only half-dressed, was shuffling closer.

"Axel," Axel repeated, laying a hand on his own breast, and there was only one response that Stefan could give.

"Tarzan," he said, pressing his hand to his own chest.

Axel laughed, and so did Stefan, and it was nice, and it was beautiful. And then Axel stepped forward, grabbed Stefan's face, kissed him far, far too chastely, and then pressed his forehead to Stefan's and said, "Date me."

Stefan wasn't shocked. He had been braced for it. He had been ready to say *no, sorry, that's not me.* But a realization struck him right then, and so instead of rejecting Axel, he quietly declared, "I'm already dating you."

"*Just* me," Axel clarified, silver eyes twinkling. A part of Stefan's soul, the part that didn't want to be tied down, the part that remembered what it felt like to love people and never wanted to love and lose again, begged him to back out right then.

But he didn't want to stop seeing Axel, and so he grabbed the taller man's wrists and squeezed. "I'm already dating *just* you. Don't tell me *you* cheated. Your majesty, I'm hurt."

Axel let out a noise that was half a laugh, half a sigh of relief. "I haven't. I don't want to."

If Axel had said something disgustingly sweet like *I only want you,* Stefan probably would have rolled his eyes and decreed that this wasn't going to work out. But perfect Axel just smiled a princely smile, leaned down, and kissed him again.

Stefan kissed back, and while at the time his chest had been filled with a ticklish warmth that spread to every inch of his body. He would look back upon that moment with indecisive regret. On the one hand, falling in love had been wonderful. Axel had made him so, so unbelievably happy.

But at the same time, if he had only said *no,* let the love fade into nothingness, then he wouldn't have been destroyed later. An empty heart couldn't be broken.

▽

Chapter
FIVE

1943

Base Twelve was little more than a tiny, abandoned house that looked more like a tiny, abandoned shed situated in the midst of the forest. Who had lived there before Papa Fox had discovered it and made it into one of his drop-off zones was anyone's guess. Probably a drug dealer of some variety. Evidently not a very successful drug dealer if the state of the place was anything to go by: the roof was full of leaks, the walls were thin enough that the Big Bad Wolf probably could have knocked the whole thing over with a tiny sneeze, and the windows were shattered.

It probably said something quite bad about Stefan's life that he could declare with utmost earnestness that he'd lived in worse.

"I'm gonna check the perimeter," said One-Twenty almost as soon as they stumbled inside, jabbing the barrel of his rifle towards one giant hole in the wall. Stefan shook his head and gestured to the most intact piece of furniture in the entire house: an old rocking chair that probably could have qualified as a booby trap.

"Sit, for fuck's sake, kid," Stefan commanded. "You haven't slept for six days straight."

One-Twenty huffed, pouted, and rubbed his eyes like an overtired toddler. "Don't call me kid. I've *told* you not to do that, Five."

"Can't remember your number half the time. The alternative is for me to call you Russkie, Russkie."

"Fine, anything but *kid*. Call me a dirty Christ-killer if you want."

"I'm damn offended, kid. How do you know *I'm* not a Jew?"

"Hitler's more Jewish than you."

"Ha!" Stefan knelt down and pulled up a loose floorboard, yanking out a small box of supplies. Whatever it was wouldn't be lifesaving, but it would get them through the night at least.

"Look, goodies!" Stefan said, opening the box and chucking the least dented can at One-Twenty's skull. He had learned long ago that one of the best benefits offered by the Contract was that anything he ate down in his Zone would stave off hunger in the real world. If he had been completely cynical and gave up entirely on the world, he could have conceivably buried himself alive and simply remained in the Zone.

Stefan didn't want to abandon the world yet, though, awful as it was, and so the Zone-meals were a real benefit in his quest to make Earth Nazi-free. His comrades were shocked by how long Stefan could apparently go without eating. Stefan himself often pretended to eat simply to allay their concerns. He certainly wasn't going to use their life-saving rations when he didn't have to.

"Eat something, damn it," Stefan said as One-Twenty checked to make sure that the can wasn't puffed up from botulism. "I don't wanna have to deal with Eight-Sixty sobbing if you fall over and starve. Ah, look!"

Stefan yanked a bottle of vodka from the depths of the box. It had likely been left behind to disinfect wounds or something useful like that, but at the moment, Stefan had a restless Russian that needed to be convinced to sit and relax. The vodka would do well for that.

"Thank God! Give it here," begged One-Twenty with a smile and an eager gleam in his eyes that reminded Stefan of the look Gerhard had offered whenever he got him a new part for their model railway. "If I have to subsist on beer for the rest of the war, I'm gonna shoot myself. You Germans are so weak, I'm surprised you don't get drunk on grape juice."

"Sit, drink, leave at least half of it," Stefan commanded, handing One-Twenty the bottle and digging through the rest of the box's meager offerings. Base Twelve had no radio, which meant that they wouldn't be able to contact Papa Fox until they made it back to the Bunker, but fortunately, it seemed that the last smuggler had left behind an updated map of the area. While One-Twenty plopped down in the rocking chair and guzzled vodka like an absolute stereotype, Stefan tried to plot out their route back to Black Fox One's hideout.

"Ah, piss," muttered Stefan after studying the map for a few moments.

"What's wrong?" queried One-Twenty, smiling like a little boy as he rocked back and forth and took another swig of precious vodka. Damn Russkie was definitely going to down more than half the bottle.

"Fucking Nazis built a new camp near here," Stefan said, holding up the map and gesturing to a spot danger-ously close to Base Twelve where the scout had sketched several symbols indicating as much.

"There's a rail not far from here, that's not shocking,"

muttered One-Twenty, gesturing with the bottle in the vague direction of where the railway cut through the land. "Probably a transit camp."

"Probably. Scout says it's small," Stefan said, gesturing to the tiny details written on the map by whichever Black Fox had left it. "Still, we might wanna take the long way around and be on the lookout for escapees we can snatch."

"Right," said One-Twenty, setting the vodka bottle at his feet and stretching his arms. "Rest here for a little and then keep moving?"

"You get outta taking a long nap just this once, but as soon as we're far from the camp, you're going down for eight straight hours if I have to knock you out myself."

"Sure thing, Five," chuckled One-Twenty. "I'll take first watch."

"Oh no! You do that and I'm never getting you to sleep. Shut your eyes, *I'll* take first watch."

One-Twenty grumbled something about Five being just like Eight-Sixty (that offended Stefan far more than being called a faggot), but he obeyed nonetheless, refusing to lie down but leaning back and shutting his eyes. A faint snoring soon filled the less-than-safe safehouse as the exhausted Russian dozed off.

It might have been easy enough for Stefan to flit down to the Zone for a little while and pass the time torturing his Subjects. If he had set the Zone's time differently, then he could have a hundred years to romp about in Hell, setting Nazis on fire or turning them inside out, while only one mere second passed on Earth.

But Stefan refused to do that, instead keeping the Zone time set one-to-one with Earth. It was less confusing that way, and also much safer. Spending what he would perceive to be thousands of years as a God, and then suddenly being dragged back to Earth? It would be disorienting, and he would almost certainly have forgotten how to shoot.

Besides, he had read enough fables to know that it was best to approach something like the Contract with caution. If he didn't use it in moderation, he might not only forget how to shoot. Anyone who spent too long with that sort of power would almost certainly forget how to be human.

So he simply sat, cradling his rifle, keeping watch like a normal human.

"Hey, I slept, so you have to eat."

Fortunately (or maybe unfortunately), One-Twenty didn't leave Stefan sitting around without anything to do for very long. Stefan smiled at the kid and shrugged, stretching his limbs.

"Not hungry, but I'll have a wink of sleep," he said, and fortunately, One-Twenty accepted that compromise. With an assurance that One-Twenty wouldn't let Stefan sleep for very long, the God of Zone N-74 shut his eyes and delved into Hell.

Stefan landed, as he always did, on his silver throne and quickly marched outside. Stefan didn't know any Master aside from Gedaliah personally, but he could only assume that certain Masters had certain preferences. No doubt many went right to the standard lake of fire. Maybe a few preferred to exclusively use Commands, which would have been perfectly acceptable as a form of torture. If Stefan's Subjects were to be believed, there was nothing more painful than a Command.

Despite this, Stefan himself didn't like to use Commands. Not out of any concern for his evil Subjects' well-being, of course. There was just something faintly… off-putting about them. It was creepy as Hell and made him sympathize with God at least a smidgeon. He now knew why God didn't just use His overwhelming power to *make* Hitler become a lovely human being. Something about forcing his will onto another human felt deeply, deeply wrong no matter how much they deserved it, and so Stefan refrained from using Commands.

Which was all well and good. Stefan wasn't the most creative human on the planet, but he had enough violent fantasies that he could torture his Subjects just fine without Commands.

And so for a while, he stood in the woods, watching as a gaggle of Jews he had summoned (soulless props, effectively extremely realistic marionettes) beat his Subjects to death over and over and over again. Each time they died, Stefan brought them back so they could be hacked to pieces all over again.

Stefan would have thought that enduring such an ordeal even once would drive a man to madness, but the Subjects always seemed to recover quickly once the torture was actually over. Perhaps dead men couldn't go mad, or perhaps (even more distressingly) the Contract made it impossible for them to lose their minds.

Stefan's sanity had been in the shitter long before he'd become a God, and while he didn't consider himself a sadist or a sociopath, he would have never denied the fact that he felt great satisfaction whenever a creature he hated felt pain. Be it a spider whose legs he ripped off as a lad or a communist he punched when he was in the SA.

Maybe that was why he had been selected to be a Master despite his relative lack of creativity. Maybe a poet or an artist would be more inclined to wince in disgust if they tore a limb off a Subject, but Stefan, who had seen friends torn to pieces and had learned to *deal with it*, had only been filled with hesitant disgust the first few times he had used his powers against the Nazis.

And every time that stupid, naive little part of him that actually believed in *do onto others* and *be kind to your enemies* would beg him to show a little bit of mercy, he would remember his friends, their screams, the pits of dead children, and that would be all the reminder he needed that these monsters deserved exactly what he was giving them.

And so he kept at it, sometimes looking away when the gore became too much, sometimes muting their screams if they started to strike at his soul, but he kept at it because it was right. *Fuck them.*

Just as he was about to revive one of his Subjects again, however, Stefan felt a horrid *tug* like he was a mountain climber that had fallen from a cliffside and barely been saved by a rope. Then, he was back in Base Twelve. One-Twenty was literally kicking him awake.

"Five, get up, come on!"

Stefan might have been a little upset by the violent awakening if he didn't look up and immediately see the reason One-Twenty hadn't been able to shake his superior awake with his hands.

One-Twenty was holding a skeleton with skin: a bald, starved child. Stefan could only tell it was a girl because she was wearing a black-and-white striped dress.

"Concentration camp escapee," One-Twenty said, and Stefan nodded numbly, his eyes pinned on a yellow triangle stuck above the skeletal girl's heart. At first, he thought that it might simply be a camp badge, but the tell-tale warm thrum that he felt as he gathered her into his arms informed him that the child was a fellow Master.

—— ▽ ——

Chapter
SIX

Before

S o, fine, he fell in love. He was careful not to be gross about it: no hand holding or bouquets or talking about their *feelings*. If he was going to be in love, it was still going to be a rush. They were still going to screw like rabbits basically everywhere except the car— broom closet, Axel's apartment, or the very great outdoors. Their dates wouldn't be nice dinners or pleasant strolls; they would be fast drives through the city peppered with stops at the local synagogue so they could chuck stones and insults at the little Jewish kids.

All that being said, Stefan would have been lying if he had declared that he didn't care at all for the quieter side of being in love. Even Stefan Harkel needed a break every once in a while, and Axel's little apartment became a pleasant little refuge of sorts.

Axel tried (and failed) to improve his cooking skills for Stefan's sake, which he appreciated both because of the thoughtfulness and because Axel's failures gave him plenty of ammunition for teasing. Stefan no longer awkwardly slept *on* Axel's arm, but actually *in* his arms. He and Axel could screw all day, sure, but they could also talk long into the night, and he knew he was in love with Axel because that fact became just as important as the amazing sex.

It wasn't until Axel took Stefan to meet his family, however, that he realized what he had with Axel wasn't just love, it was full-on vomit-inducing *true love*. Love was one thing. You could love someone even if they only knew a few things about you. But if you revealed what a mess you were, and they didn't run away screaming, that was *true love*. The sort of love that made people *stupid*.

Stefan had legitimately thought that Axel was telling a joke when he asked him to come to his parents' house a few days after Hitler lost his 1932 bid for the German presidency. Stefan laughed. Axel didn't laugh back and instead just smiled that damn princely smile of his. It was only then that Stefan realized his idiot boyfriend was being serious.

"My father's upset about the election. Throwing dinners makes him feel better," Axel explained. "My sisters will be there, my mother, and I know for a fact that my little brother and his wife will *not* be there, so you won't have to worry about vomiting."

"You've gotta be kidding me, Axel." Stefan half laughed, and half sighed because a romantic ride into the countryside was one thing, but this…whatever this was, this pathetic imitation of a ritual reserved for heterosexuals. *Hey, Mama, Papa, there's this person I like. Can I have them over for dinner?*

No. He wasn't going to go to Axel's house and sit there and smile and pretend to be Axel's *really close friend*.

"My parents have a dog. Sonne. Golden retriever," Axel said, his smirk curling in an insufferably adorable way. "He's *really* cute."

Goddamn it.

He went, and he smiled when Axel introduced him as Stefan Harkel, his *really good friend* from the Brownshirts. Axel hadn't been kidding when he said that he was the son of a rich man; the Lahner manor was the size of several apartment complexes smashed together, and Herr Paul Lahner himself just reeked of old money. From his ornately sculpted beard and moustache, to his crystal-studded watch, to his damn golden *monocle* with a diamond-encrusted chain.

Still, Paul Lahner seemed like a nice fellow. If Stefan hadn't known how deeply Axel insisted on staying in the closet for fear of humiliating his parents, he might have even liked him.

It definitely seemed like Axel had a more tender relationship with his parents and his siblings than Stefan had ever had with his family. Not that Stefan's family had been *terrible* except for the whole nearly-beating-him-to-death thing. Stefan's mother had been strict, but that had been born out of love, out of fear that her children would go to Hell when they died if she didn't beat them into good little Christians. (Later, Stefan sometimes wanted to track her down and boast that he was so un-Christian that he got to go to Hell while he was still alive, but he honestly didn't want to hear her scream at him again.)

Stefan's father had been paternal but not soft: willing to smack his son upside the head and give him the occasional fatherly embrace, but never to the point where Stefan would have described him as *tender*.

Axel's family, on the other hand, was tenderness personified. Hardly had Axel entered his family's sprawling living room when Paul Lahner leapt from his cozy chair and enveloped his son in a hug. "There's my boy!" he shouted, ruffling Axel's hair and even kissing his forehead.

Axel's mother was very much the same, hugging him, kissing his face, and fretting about how underfed he looked. Axel's two sisters all but fought over who got to hug their beloved big brother first, an argument that was settled when he took one sister into each arm and lifted them both into the air.

Stefan could see why Axel was utterly terrified of losing a family like this. It had been hard enough for him to lose his family, and the Harkels had never been as close as this.

Stefan busied himself with Sonne the golden retriever, who was well worth the awkwardness with his big, dumb, slobbery smile and intense, world-class begging stare. Stefan sat at the table, sneaking the dog scraps from his meal (which was utterly delicious and made him realize why Axel had never learned to cook.) He did his best to be a relatively mum guest, which was easy since Paul Lahner was a chatterbox who dominated the conversation with talk of Hitler and the damn Jews rigging the election against him.

"This entire democracy facade is utterly useless," Paul ranted. "The masses can't be trusted to pick their leaders when they've been subjected to the lying Jew press for so many years! Even *if* it was a fair election, which I doubt, Hitler wouldn't be able to get in with all these idiots clogging up the polling booths."

"Tell us how you really feel, Papa," chuckled Axel, earning a laugh and a fond slap on the shoulder from the older gentleman.

"I feel terrible that you and your friend here have been working so hard for the Cause, and yet you have to see it bear no fruit."

"We've definitely been working hard," Axel said, shooting a little wink across the table at Stefan.

"Herr Harkel, what do you think about the presidential fiasco?" Paul asked, and Stefan hastily tried to pretend like he hadn't just fed the dog about half a steak, clearing his throat and shrugging.

"I agree with you: people are stupid. I think Hitler just needs to forget about trying to work within this democracy and overthrow it. We never wanted it, after all. It was forced onto us by the Jews at Versailles."

Stefan hoped that sounded smart, because even if Paul Lahner would obviously never approve of his and Axel's relationship, it was clear that Axel loved his father dearly. Stefan didn't want to screw things up right away by making a bad impression. Quite fortunately, Paul Lahner made a noise of agreement and wagged an approving finger at his guest.

"Right you are, Herr Harkel, right you are! Democracy is just another tool for the Jews to control us while we sit around thinking *we're* in charge. I understand why Hitler feels the need to try and work within this system after what happened in '23, but Mussolini didn't become Il Duce by asking politely. And dear Hitler has far more insidious forces working against him! Look how the lying Jew press besmirches the reputation of the SA, painting them as nothing but degenerate rabble-rousers!"

Stefan saw Axel's shoulders stiffen, saw his smile become crooked.

"You can't trust a word that the papers say about anything," Stefan said hastily. "All the editors are Jews. Anyway, you shouldn't let the results of the election get you too upset, Herr Lahner. We should all have faith in Hitler."

"Absolutely, absolutely!" Paul said, patting Axel's shoulder. "Axel, your friend here is a smart fellow! Good on you for bringing decent company home! I'm sick of entertaining guests that don't *get it*. Love your sister-in-law, but she truly doesn't understand the Jewish Question!"

"I'm glad to be here, sir," Stefan said, offering a toast towards the chortling philanthropist. Axel's eyes glistened.

"We're most certainly happy to have you, Stefan. Although…" Frau Lahner gave her son a look that was shockingly similar to the one Sonne was currently giving Stefan. "I will admit that when Axel said he was bringing a guest along, I was hoping it would be a lovely lady."

Axel laughed a hollow laugh and smiled that princely perfect smile even though Stefan could see that a part of him wanted to scream. "Mama, don't tell Stefan he isn't lovely, you'll hurt his feelings!"

Everyone laughed, including Stefan, because of course it was a joke. Ha ha. Very funny.

"I don't mean to offend, Stefan," Frau Lahner assured her guest sweetly. "I just want as many grandbabies as possible!"

"No offense taken, ma'am." *Bitch.*

The conversation turned back to politics after that, and Stefan was the perfect house guest. He smiled when he was supposed to, fed the dog the rest of his meal because his gut was writhing, and drank more than he was wont to because he needed to.

Stefan could sense when he was just past his limit on wine, however. He didn't like to drink to excess, not because of any sort of inclination towards moderation (*ha*) but because he knew what he was like when he was drunk. Not violent or horny or anything fun; a drunk Stefan was a sad Stefan, and he knew he was getting drunk when he looked at Axel chatting happily with his parents and started to hate him, just a little.

Stefan tried to remember the last time he'd shared a meal with his family and hated that he couldn't.

Still, he was good. Good and nice and polite and *quiet.* The hours marched on slowly until at last a plastered Paul Lahner declared that they all needed to turn in. Axel said that he was going to show Stefan to his room, and Axel's perfect family all bade their guest goodnight. Sonne trotted upstairs with Axel and Stefan, having decided that he liked the indulgent guest better than anyone else.

"Here we are," Axel said, ushering Stefan and Sonne into one grand guest room. He entered himself, shutting and locking the door behind them.

"Sorry I can't stay the night," Axel said with a wink. "My parents sleep on the other side of the house, so we should be good to talk, but nothing besides that."

"I don't need you. I have Sonne, and he's more handsome," Stefan declared, plopping down on the bed and patting the space beside him. The dog panted happily and jumped right up, licking Stefan's face. His breath was terrible, but Stefan didn't care.

"Errr…darling, the dog's not supposed to be on the bed," Axel chuckled.

"'Darling'?" Stefan snorted. "Never call me that again or I'll out you in front of your parents."

"I…hm…please don't joke about that." Axel leaned against the door as though he wanted to blockade it just in case his father came bursting in and found them flirting. Stefan felt like a snake was coiled inside his chest.

"All right," Stefan said, his tone making it clear that he did not feel *all right*. He desperately wanted Axel to drop it right there, say goodnight, leave him to cuddle with the adorable dog and maybe cry a little into Sonne's tangled golden fur.

But stupid Axel instead pushed himself off the door and stepped slightly closer to his boyfriend. "Hey," he said, his voice somehow at once gentle and firm. "You were kind of glaring at me halfway through dinner."

"Was I?" Stefan was well aware that his voice was too high pitched to sound truly casual.

"I know you hate…well, hiding. You did a good job, and I appreciate it a lot."

"Good. Wouldn't wanna fuck up your *perfect* relationship with your *perfect* family," Stefan said, the booze flowing through his veins and forcing bitter honesty out of his throat. Axel winced.

"It's not that I *want* to hide you. I really wish that I didn't have to…" Axel confessed quietly. He sat on the bed, on the other side of Sonne. For a moment, there was silence between the two of them, the only noise being Sonne's happy pants as he was pet by both men.

Drop it, drop it, drop it.

Axel didn't. "My relationship with my family isn't perfect. No family is perfect. I imagine yours wasn't perfect."

Dropitdropitdropitdropit…

"Stefan, what *is* your family like? You've never talked about them."

Fuck him and his stupid, magnetic silver eyes. And fuck Paul Lahner too for plying Stefan with fine wine and forcing him to be honest.

"I haven't talked about them because I haven't seen them since I was sixteen!"

He hoped Axel, who must have known the consequences of exiting the closet given how thoroughly he feared stepping a toe out of it, would simply fill in the blanks. But instead Axel affixed Stefan with that soft, genuine look and said, "Tell me."

Stefan didn't want to. He had never told anyone. Not Wilhelm, not his friends, nobody.

But he and Axel were in a relationship. *Exclusive.* Boyfriends. That meant they had to talk, and not just about cars or dogs or how great Hitler was. No, they had to *talk* talk. About deep, meaningful, important shit like Stefan's family and how much he hated them and how much he missed them and how sometimes he wished he'd been less sloppy and stayed in the closet so he could have a sliver of what Axel had.

And Stefan *really* didn't want to talk about it, because if he talked about it, he'd have to think about it. And nothing could hurt him if he just didn't think about it and punched or fucked someone instead.

But Axel didn't want to fuck, there weren't any Jews or communists to punch, and Stefan had gone past his threshold for how many drinks he could have without spiraling.

So he talked about it. And he tried to talk about it in a tone of utter indifference because he might have been a queer, but he wasn't a weak, effeminate, pathetic little stereotype. He was strong, a fighter, and nothing affected him, and he didn't give a shit, and he didn't want Axel to think less of him even though he *didn't care*.

He had to *not care* because it wasn't like there was a damn thing he could do about it anyway, so if he cared, he was hurt. And if he was hurt, then he was weak and helpless. And then *he* was the loser, and *fuck that*. It was easier to just pretend like he felt nothing until he really did feel nothing.

And so as Stefan told his story, he shrugged and sighed and rolled his eyes like he was describing the time his father had chastised him for playing with matches when he was eight years old. And Axel just listened until he was done, his expression utterly neutral.

"I see," Axel said at last, and Stefan would have ended things right then if he had detected even a hint of pity in his boyfriend's voice, but there wasn't any. He sounded angry. That…that was nice, because it all made Stefan angry deep down, and it was good to know that he wasn't completely alone.

"That was fucking shitty," Axel said, reaching forward

and running his fingers through Sonne's golden locks. "That was a shitty thing to do, both of 'em."

"Yeah?" Stefan said. "And you think your folks wouldn't do the same thing if they knew you were fucking me?"

"Oh, I'm sure they would," Axel said in a rather casual tone, not a second of hesitation. "They say parents love their children unconditionally, but that's bullshit. No love's unconditional. There's always a compromise to make or a secret to keep. This, what I like, that's mine. I just…"

Axel rolled Sonne onto his back and started giving the dog slow, contemplative belly rubs. "I love them, that's the problem," he muttered. "My parents. I love them, and I'd love them even if they did that to me, and I'm sure they'd still love me as much as they'd hate me. It's all easier like this. Everyone's happy, nobody has to lose anything."

Axel stopped petting the dog and looked at Stefan, silver eyes glistening with outright admiration. "If what happened to you happened to me, I don't know what I'd do. Probably shoot myself. You're really damn strong, you know that?"

Fuck him for being so perfect. Stefan tried his best to keep a sob from ripping out of his lungs, but he failed.

"Stefan?"

"I love them too, that's…" he hiccupped. "I still love them. I fucking hate them, but I love them. I loved them and they…couldn't they have just pretended like they didn't see anything? I think they thought I was gonna hurt Gerhard. I wouldn't do that; I fucking loved that kid. I wasn't a good son, but I was a decent son, and I was a great brother, and they didn't even let me say goodbye to him…"

"Stefan…"

Sober Stefan would have laughed in drunk Stefan's

face right then as he started gasping in an attempt to prevent ugly sobs from ripping out of his throat. Axel stopped petting Sonne and traversed the bed, sitting on Stefan's other side and yanking him into a half-hug while the dog, confused and eager to cheer his new friend up, started trying to lick Stefan's tears away.

"They probably fed him some bullshit and told him I was a pervert who tried to touch him," Stefan said once he had caught his breath. "He probably fucking hates me."

"Maybe not," Axel suggested softly. "Maybe he remembers you enough."

"Maybe...*blagh! Sonne!*"

The golden retriever managed to lick the inside of Stefan's mouth as he began to answer Axel's hopeful suggestion, making Stefan spit and laugh and cry all at once.

"Damn dog," Axel chuckled.

"He's a good dog," Stefan said, scratching the grinning golden retriever's chin. "We had a dog, me and Gerhard. Pup named Arvin. We'd play in the backyard together, toss a ball between us and make the dog run for it. He used to sleep in my bed because I didn't have a frame, just a mattress on the floor. He'd wake me up because he always had dog dreams where he'd be chasing something. I think he was chasing Gerhard in his sleep because he never caught up to him in real life."

"Sounds like a good dog."

"He was. My parents locked him up in the bathroom the day they kicked me out. I heard him barking and crying. It was..." Stefan bit his lip and tried to focus on the happy dog before him, so he didn't have to think too much about the sound Arvin had made that day.

"Worst noise I've ever heard. Never should have been that sad. He was a good boy," Stefan muttered after a moment, once more failing to stop a sob from clawing its way out of his chest. "Is it weird that I sometimes feel worse about not being able to say goodbye to Arvin? He couldn't understand any of this shit. I was just gone to him."

"That's not weird," Axel assured him. Then, quieter, "*You're* not weird."

Hearing those words for the very first time in his entire life made a little burst of fireworks go off in Stefan's heart. "Thanks. Damn, I miss having a dog. Worst part about not having a home is that you can't have a dog. Dogs are great, you know. They don't give a shit what you are as long as you love them. Look."

He kissed Axel right then, partially because he wanted to, and partially to prove a point. Sonne, unsurprisingly, merely watched, wagged his tail, and drooled on the bed.

"See?" Stefan hiccupped, laughing and petting the dog. "He doesn't give a shit."

Axel nodded, squeezed Stefan once more, and then quietly proclaimed, "Dogs are great."

—————— ▽ ——————

If Axel had brought up Stefan's little sob-fest in the weeks that followed dinner with the Lahners, Stefan might have ended their relationship out of embarrassment. But Axel never brought it up. The only thing that changed was that he didn't invite Stefan to his apartment for a few weeks, which might have been concerning if he didn't double up on their drives out to the great outdoors to make up for it.

When Axel did, after one particularly fun brawl with the Bolsheviks, finally ask Stefan to come over, Stefan was relieved but refused to show it. "Good. I was getting sick of grass."

Axel let out a small hum. His silver eyes were cloudy

like tarnished treasure, and his lips were pursed in a thin line. He shifted to and fro like he had a rock in his boot. If Stefan hadn't known Axel well, he might have assumed that his boyfriend wanted to invite him over to have a break-up talk. A private little *it's not you, it's me.*

But Axel would have never been so cruel. If he didn't want to continue, he wouldn't have played games.

"Are you all right?" Stefan asked. If Axel didn't want to break up, then maybe something bad had happened to his family, or maybe he needed to transfer out of Vogel's Troop.

Axel didn't respond for a moment, as though he couldn't even hear his lover through the din of his own thoughts, but then he shook his head and said, "I'm fine. Just, uh, just please come over tonight."

"I'll be there, don't worry," Stefan assured him, patting his boyfriend's shoulder and refraining from kissing him only because they were in public, and he knew how Axel felt about that. Axel must have sensed Stefan's act of self-control because he briefly patted his hand and gave him a real, gentle smile.

"Good, that's…good…" Axel walked away after that, still seemingly in a fog.

Stefan returned to Wilhelm's barracks, received a very nice fatherly hug from Wilhelm for his good work against the Reds, freshened up, and then rushed to Axel's apartment.

He knocked on the door, and before it was even opened, Stefan was greeted by a sound that made his heart do a little backflip: "*Bark, bark, bark!*"

"Down, boy!" came Axel's voice as he opened up the door, greeting Stefan with a warm smile while barely holding back a small brown dog with floppy ears and a tail that wagged so energetically that it was a wonder it didn't fall right off. The dog struggled to leap upon

Stefan, who skittered inside the apartment and knelt down.

"Don't worry," Axel chuckled, releasing the mutt, who immediately started licking Stefan's cheeks. "Stole one'a your socks and made sure he got used to your scent."

"You got a dog!" Stefan yelped with delight, scratching the smiling mutt behind his ears. Axel didn't say anything for a minute, and when he did, his words made Stefan's heart stop.

"I got *us* a dog."

Stefan had not been braced for that, and so he stayed on the ground for a moment, squeezing his eyes shut as the dog licked every inch of his face, until he finally remembered how to control his own body and lifted his head out of the dog's reach, staring at Axel.

Axel was still squirming and shifting his weight and making a face like his own tongue had turned into a venomous snake, but eventually he unleashed a shuddering breath and offered Stefan a hand and a plea: "Live with me."

Once again, that little part of Stefan's soul that was reasonable and not driven by hormones and love begged him to say *no, no, no, I'm not getting in this deep.*

But the simple fact of the matter was that he did love Axel, and even though his offer was too good to be true and Stefan Harkel was far too unlucky a man to ever have this sort of fortune, he decided to go for it regardless. "I was already living with you most of the time until a few weeks ago."

"I'm sorry," chuckled Axel, grabbing Stefan's hand and lifting him to his feet. He nudged his head down to the wiggly dog that scurried around the two men's feet and said, "I needed to…well…get him. And I needed to think."

"And you're sure you've thought enough?" Stefan said,

squeezing Axel's hand tight. "What about your parents? I won't make you parade around, but I won't live in an apartment while you go off and get into a lavender marriage…"

"I know!" Axel winced at his own yelp of frustration, then gazed at Stefan with apologetic softness. "I know… I…I'll think of something. I'll say I want to be celibate, or pretend I got injured. I don't care, I…"

If Axel had gotten down on one knee and proclaimed his eternal love for Stefan right then and there, Stefan would have ended things on the spot. Instead, he just grabbed Stefan's other hand, squeezed until Stefan was certain his fingers would break, and confessed, "I don't want this to end."

Stefan yanked his hands from Axel's grasp because it hurt, not because he was refusing, and closed the distance between them. "Me neither," he said, putting his hands on Axel's hips and kissing him briefly, like they really were a damn married couple.

"I wish you were a woman," Axel sighed somewhat bitterly even as he smiled.

"If I was a woman, you wouldn't want this," Stefan pointed out with a smirk, and Axel nodded.

"I know…" Axel pressed his forehead against Stefan's. "I just…"

"You *do* want this, right?" Stefan asked, the query almost clogging his throat because he wanted this and didn't want Axel to take it back.

Axel's response was so quiet that he almost didn't hear it even though their faces were pressed together. "Too much."

———————— ▽ ————————

Chapter
SEVEN

The second time that Stefan had been sent to Dachau, he had encountered a familiar face in the form of the one the guards—either an old friend or someone he'd screwed before Axel, he hadn't been able to remember the exact details. Either way, for the rest of Stefan's short second visit, that guard whose name he couldn't remember had stopped by every morning to give Stefan a share of his own rations: eggs, sausage, the things men in Dachau literally killed each other for.

Stefan hadn't eaten a crumb of it at first. Instead, he had found the most emaciated man branded with a pink triangle and gave it all to him (after assuring him that this wasn't a bribe, that he didn't want sex in exchange for another day of survival.) The man had cried and thanked him and called him an angel, and for a moment, Stefan had felt like one.

Until the man died, and one of the other prisoners who had been a doctor once examined him and said that he'd died because he'd eaten too much too quickly after subsisting on bread laced with wood shavings for too long. Because the human body was so poorly and cruelly designed that giving it food when it was a skeleton with skin didn't save it, it just sealed its fate.

That was the only time Stefan had ever thought of actively killing himself, as opposed to killing himself by being so rebellious and stupid that death was inevitable. Suicide by poor choices was his preferred way to go, not running into the nearest electrified fence.

It was a good life lesson, though, because One-Twenty probably would have killed the skeletal child that he carried into Base Twelve right away if Stefan hadn't remembered that man from Dachau and stopped the Russian from giving her all of their food.

"Here, here, sweetie…" Stefan said in a voice so gentle and comforting that if Eight-Sixty had been there, the idiot probably would have patted him on the back. One-Twenty tore off his coat and laid it on the hard floor to soften it.

"All right, here, don't worry. We're Black Foxes, we're gonna help you," Stefan assured her, laying her on the Russian's coat. He unscrewed the cap on his water canteen and lifted it to her bruised lips.

The girl's eyes, which seemed to take up half of her hollow face, were not focused on him as she struggled to drink, but on the Contract over his heart.

"M-Master…" she whimpered. One-Twenty let out a feral growl as he paced frantically back and forth.

"Those animals…those damn animals…" the Russian hissed.

"Please, have to…" the girl begged, glancing down at the Contract on her breast and whimpering desperately.

"One-Twenty, go out and search the perimeter again," Stefan ordered. "See if there are any other escapees or any guards coming after her."

"Right!" Thankfully, One-Twenty's rebellious streak had restricted itself to chasing Viktor Naden. He obeyed Stefan's orders immediately, leaving the two Masters to discuss their heavenly secret in confidence.

"Pen...pencil...something...p-please..." the girl gasped, her exhausted eyes flitting about frantically. Stefan, who always carried a writing utensil specifically for this purpose, pulled a pencil from his pocket.

"Do you want me to...?"

"No, I have to..." With a Herculean amount of strength, the girl who seemed too weak to even bear her own scant weight sat up, her bony fingers wrapping around the pencil.

"I can help," Stefan said. It was awful to watch her hands shake, to see how every slight movement took so much willpower. She made a small, rebuking squeak.

"Has to...me only...no help..." She plucked the yellow triangle from her breast and unfurled it across her knees. There was a desperate aura consuming her, as though the world itself would end if she didn't complete this task before...

Stefan swallowed, gritted his teeth, and forced himself to care a little less because he could sense that trying to parent her right then would be fruitless and damaging.

"I renounce the Contract to Zone N-1..." The girl struck through her tidy signature at the bottom of the paper. The Contract glowed gold.

"I renounce...the Contract to Zone N-1..." She crossed out her name again. There was a more intense golden glow. The pencil almost fell out of her hands, but she held on, her soft blue eyes glowing with resolve. A part of Stefan wanted to say something. Eight-Sixty would have. *You're doing a great job,* some shit like that, but that would probably be awfully patronizing to a girl that had clearly overcome worse than flourishing a dull pencil.

"I renounce...the Contract to Zone...N-1..." One more weak strike of the pencil and a blinding glow consumed the Contract. When the light faded, her struck-through name was gone, and the Contract was blank, fresh, ready for a new Master.

"Sign it, please...*please*..." Her desperate tone drove Stefan to act without thought, without even glancing at the new Contract that he was accepting. He took the pencil from her and signed his name on the newly blank spot on the bottom of the paper. A burst of power more intense than the one he had felt when he'd first accepted his Contract from Ha-Satan consumed his body before settling on his soul, leaving him anxiously exhilarated.

One tiny hand wrapped around his wrist.

"Camp...Kommandant...he's a Master...so many Contracts...Grandmaster..." the girl explained, and it was clear that speaking at all was agonizing for her.

"He did this to you," Stefan said. She made a small, affirmative noise.

"Transit camp...finds Masters...makes them give him Contract...torture...he can't...he *can't* get Nazi-Land, this one, no matter what, promise me..."

"I promise," Stefan said, making sure that his voice was resolute. She gave him a small smile that was at once beautiful and painful.

"You were so brave to do this," Stefan said, giving into his inner Eight-Sixty and grasping her little hand in his. "You're a good girl. What's your name?"

"A-Alice."

"Don't worry, Alice. We'll take it from here. You don't have anything to worry about. Everything's gonna be okay. You're gonna be fine."

Stefan had been told more than once that he was good at this sort of thing: giving last words of comfort to the dying, being a rock to lean on while they passed away.

That praise had been uttered by his companions with awe, but really, he was a bit offended that they thought so little of him that they were surprised when he wasn't an ass to a dying man, much less a dying little girl. He was an asshole to the living, not the dead or the dying, not unless they had it coming.

Besides, it was easy to be confident and strong in the face of death when he knew for a fact that angels existed, that they would see to it that the innocent were comforted and the guilty punished.

So the girl, Alice, died with a smile and a sigh of relief. He stayed kneeling beside her for a moment, waiting for the numb feeling to fade into anger so he could dive into whatever Zone she had given him and torture the fuck out of whatever Subjects he now owned.

One-Twenty stumbled in eventually. It might have been five minutes or five hours after she went. Stefan couldn't tell sometimes.

"Is she…?"

Stefan nodded and let her hand slip from his fingers. One-Twenty let out a noise that was part snarl, part choke.

"Animals!" the Russian hissed. "When I get my hands on them, God as my witness…!"

Stefan really wanted to say, *I'm not sure God is your witness right now,* but instead he said, "I don't know if she was a Jew, but I'd guess she was. We'll bury her, and you can give her rites in Hebrew."

One-Twenty nodded, clenching his fists and muttering something in either Hebrew or Yiddish, probably some sort of curse, maybe a plea to God that He wouldn't be answering. Stefan knew that God didn't observe the affairs of Hell, but sometimes it felt like He was just as blind to what occurred on Earth.

Speaking of Hell…

One-Twenty gathered Alice into his arms with utmost tenderness and carried her outside, inviting Stefan to join him for her funeral as soon as he was done collecting himself.

Hardly had One-Twenty stepped out of the dilapidated little house when Stefan took a deep breath to fan the flame raging in his soul and finally looked down at the paper.

His heart almost stopped. There was only one name on the Contract.

**THE LORD HAS GIVEN THEE
A POWER KNOWN TO ONLY HE
THE POWER OF COMPLETE CONTROL
OVER THIS, A HUMAN SOUL
UNTIL THE MOMENT OF REPENTANCE
AND THE END OF THEIR SENTENCE**

**THE ONE WHO SIGNS THIS
CONTRACT
IS HEREBY THE MASTER OF
<u>ZONE N-1</u>
AND THE FOLLOWING SOULS CONFINED
THEREIN:**
Reinhard Tristan Eugen Heydrich

———————— ▽ ————————

Chapter EIGHT

Stefan Harkel's life had been absolutely perfect until Reinhard Heydrich fucked it all up.

Granted, it wasn't all Heydrich. He wasn't even sure if it was *mostly* Heydrich. Maybe it was 40 percent Heydrich, 50 percent Himmler, 7 percent Goering, 2.5 percent Hitler, and then from there it was a scattering of little nobodies making up the other .5 percent.

And really, even if it *had* been all Heydrich's fault, even if Heydrich had personally gone to every SA trooper's house and beat their skull in with a rusty rake, Stefan should have been grateful. If it hadn't been for the Night of Long Knives, he probably would have never stopped being a Nazi. Maybe he would have eventually found himself in a forest in Poland, aiming a rifle at the back of a toddler's head.

Maybe Reinhard Heydrich had saved his soul.

Whatever. Stefan was still going to torture the shit out of him.

Heydrich deserved it, after all. For what he did to innocent children as head of the *Einsatzgruppen.*

For what he did to prisoners in his capacity as the Head of the Gestapo.

For what he did to the Jews as the Mastermind of the Final Solution, the author of the death camp system.

For what he did to occupied Czechoslovakia as the Butcher of Prague—for those crimes, he had at least paid a little bit since two brave Czech agents had taken vengeance for their nation in 1942, when they had given Heydrich a death that wasn't nearly painful enough.

Of course, in Stefan's opinion, Heydrich deserved an eternity of torment for what he had done to his fellow Nazis.

Stefan had been happy. So happy. So happy that it didn't feel real because he wasn't supposed to be happy. Not really happy, not fulfilled. He had been all right with that to a certain extent, in the same way someone born without legs eventually, to preserve their sanity, decided that they preferred using a wheelchair anyway.

Broken little queers like Stefan Harkel didn't get relationships and happy holidays and cute puppies and a fulfilling domestic life. That was the way it was in the world, and for the longest time he'd thought *fine*. And maybe, *Fuck you too, world*, for good measure.

But Axel changed all of that with three words, *live with me*, and after that, they lived together, all but married, for two long, wonderful years. He and Axel were together, a family with a cute little dog that he loved almost as much as his boyfriend. (Armin became the pup's name, both because Stefan wanted to honor his old dog and because he was too uncreative to come up with anything else.)

Politically, everything was going well too. While Hitler hadn't managed to snag the role of the German President during the 1932 election, some clever political maneuvering allowed him to instead become the Chancellor in

1933. From there, he kept swiping little bits of power like a pickpocket slipping little coins from a fat purse.

The Führer gained even more power when someone lit the Reichstag on fire, leading to the Enabling Act, which effectively made Hitler a dictator even while Hindenburg was still supposedly the head of state. (Germany would be told by the Nazi press that communists had started the flames, but even at the time, Stefan was relatively certain that Hermann Goering was the culprit. Hitler's corpulent second-in-command would have had every political motivation to start a crisis in order to justify his Führer stealing emergency powers. And if it hadn't been on purpose, then maybe the perpetually drug-addled Goering had simply dropped a match in a state of morphine-induced stupidity.)

All of the Nazis' dreams were coming true. Hitler was in control. The elderly President Hindenburg was shuffling towards death's door, and once he was out of the picture, there would be no one standing in Hitler's way. Democracy was dead. The National Socialists were well on their way towards creating the utopia that they had dreamed of. Stefan Harkel, eager little fascist, was ecstatic. So was Axel. Wilhelm's hugs became longer and tighter and punctuated with hopeful little remarks about how the Cause was getting stronger by the day. Every day, it seemed, was better than the last.

And the peak of it all, which naturally was also the point of downfall, was Hitler's birthday. It was a birthday party that spread from border to border. All across Germany, cakes decorated with swastikas were served and mailboxes were stuffed with birthday cards for the Führer. Wilhelm's Troop celebrated together, and the Troop-Leader even allowed Stefan to bring Armin along.

Stefan didn't doubt that he had enjoyed Hitler's forty-fifth birthday far more than Adolf Hitler had himself. It was a day spent surrounded by those who knew him, who liked him, and in the case of Armin and Axel, who actually loved him. Surrounded by swastikas, devouring cake, barhopping with his comrades until they all returned to the SA barrack and threw a grand party. At one point, Stefan was certain that he was going to break down and cry because he was happy, and he wanted it to last forever.

"Armin's gonna get fat, darling," Axel teased, somehow ruining and solidifying the happy moment all at once. Axel had been a lot more openly frisky tonight, perhaps because they were surrounded by friends, or more likely because their friends were so drunk and loud that it was impossible for them to hear anything Axel said.

"Quit calling me that, and no he's not," Stefan said, collecting a dollop of icing into his hand and letting Armin lick it off his palm. "He's eaten less cake today than you have."

"You're such a devoted mother," cackled Axel, pinching Stefan's cheek, which earned him a slap on the wrist.

"I am *not* the fucking mother in this relationship, you bitch."

"Oooh," Axel crooned. He leaned a bit closer and whispered in a tone that sent fire shooting through Stefan's body, "Let's go home and we'll see which of us is the bitch."

Happy end to a happy day. Stefan made sure that Armin had completely cleaned his hand before he reached under the table, pinching Axel's arse and earning a small, surprised squeak from his lover. Axel blushed redder than the swastika flags surrounding them and scowled like a child that had just lost a race.

"Keep that up and I'll drag you to the damn broom closet again," Axel said, which sounded like both a threat and a promise. Stefan chuckled and stood up, gesturing to their ignorantly chipper mutt.

"Not in front of the kid," he said, offering Axel a hand and helping him to his feet.

"You two heading out?" Wilhelm chuckled with a knowing wink. Axel turned scarlet and Stefan nodded. Determined as Axel was to keep his sexuality under-wraps, their relationship was obvious enough that Wilhelm had picked up on it.

Wilhelm had never said anything, at most only indicating his knowledge with cheeky winks and chuckles and mutterings of, *You're going off with Axel to do friend things, hm, yes, very platonic.* It seemed that he approved either way, maybe because he could tell that Stefan's mood had improved since he and Axel had become inseparable.

"Dog's getting antsy," Stefan said, which was quite the bad lie because Armin, stuffed with cake and bratwurst, was lying in a puddle of his own drool in a happy-dog coma. Axel was probably going to have to carry the mutt home, maybe with the use of a crane and a crew of twelve men.

Wilhelm just rolled his eyes and laughed at the excuse. He clapped Axel on the shoulder and offered Stefan a tight paternal embrace. Stefan would always regret that he never told Wilhelm how much he loved those hugs. He would have happily given up his Contract to get just one more that he could really appreciate.

Wilhelm kept them just a bit longer to make sure they signed the birthday card that the troop was going to send to Hitler. It ended up taking twenty minutes because Stefan refused to leave until Axel consented to put some ink on the thoroughly exhausted Armin's paw so that he could "sign" it with his pawprint. Stefan doubted that Hitler would actually be reading every card that was sent to him, but it was a fun little thing to do, nonetheless. It would probably be less fun later on when he would have to wrestle the puppy into the bathtub, but Stefan Harkel lived for the moment and regretted his dumbass choices later.

Wilhelm bade farewell to his comrades, and the couple offered a cheerfully cheeky, "Happy Birthday!" to the portrait of Hitler that hung above the fireplace before they marched out into the night. Armin immediately yanked Stefan towards a patch of grass and started sniffing about for a spot to go to the bathroom.

"Ugh, it's gonna take us forever to get home," Axel sighed, glancing at a few partygoers across the street who were stumbling into a bar. "Armin's so *picky*."

"Broom closet's still an option, maybe an alleyway if we can tie up the mutt," Stefan said. "Streets are pretty bare."

"We are *not* leaving Armin tied up, you monster," Axel said, bumping against Stefan in a suggestively teasing way. "He's too cute, someone will steal him. I'm worried enough about someone stealing *you*."

"He's cuter than me," Stefan said, and of course, Armin picked that exact moment to squat down in a decidedly not-cute fashion and take a very not-cute dump in the grass.

"Told you not to feed him cake," Axel cackled cruelly when Stefan then had to clean up after their mutt, ruining his day and maybe his life.

"Fuck you, and also you," Stefan said, glaring at Armin, who panted and smiled like the brainless animal that he was. Stefan loved that damn dog almost as much as he loved Axel, and right then, even picking up shit felt good because Axel was smiling at him, and Armin was happy, and everything was just perfect.

But then Armin's big, dumb smile morphed into a growl, and he let out an aggressive bark.

"Cute dog."

A voice and a horrendous smell. Cigarettes, even worse than the kind Axel smoked, worse than the dog shit that Stefan flung into the nearest garbage can before turning towards the speaker.

A man was leaning against a lamppost decorated with swastika streamers, taking a deep draw from a foul-smelling cigarette. The first thing that Stefan noticed about him was the uniform: black with silver trimmings and a blood-red armband, pristine and unwrinkled.

An SS man, a member of Hitler's most elite army, though his greasy black hair betrayed imperfect Aryan genetics. It seemed that he took better care of his uniform than he did himself; he was fit enough, a bit short, maybe an inch or two shorter than Axel. Still, he must have been dreadfully overworked if the bags under his almond-colored eyes were anything to go by.

A weasel, that was the first thing Stefan thought as the SS man smiled a crooked smile and stepped towards them. If a weasel were turned into a man, that weasel-man would look just like the SS officer before them.

The Weasel-SS-Man tossed his cigarette onto the pavement, a bit too close to Armin. Axel took initiative and stomped it out before the dog could even think of licking it.

"Heil Hitler," the SS man said.

"Heil Hitler," replied Axel, his tone bright in a way that Stefan knew well: it was the same forcefully cheery tone he used whenever his father asked him if he'd found a nice German girl to marry yet.

"Heil," Stefan said, trying for a neutral tone himself. He didn't have many strong opinions about the SS despite the rivalry between Himmler's troops and Röhm's four-million-man strong Brownshirts.

Stefan definitely would have never joined the SS; he wouldn't have been willing to fill out a damn family tree to prove that he had three centuries' worth of pure Aryan ancestry. Their uniforms were certainly dashing, but he looked good in his brown uniform, and besides, as Axel had pointed out, the SA's apparel matched Hitler's aesthetics. The Führer had never donned the black tunic of Himmler's legion.

Besides, every SS man that Stefan had ever encountered was weird. Case in point: the one in front of him.

"The Führer's birthday was really something, wasn't it?" the SS man chuckled. "You gentlemen enjoyed yourselves?"

"Plenty," said Stefan, crossing his arms. "Dog ate too much cake, though."

"Aha!" chuckled the SS man. "Certainly shows how much we owe the Führer, doesn't it? A few years ago, we couldn't even give bread to children, and now we can give cake to dogs."

"Right..." muttered Axel. That was the other reason Stefan would never be joining the SS. Sure, he was a fascist. Sure, he liked Hitler. Sure, he was a National Socialist. But he was more than just that, and the SA men were too. They were people first, and tools of Nazism second.

Meanwhile, every SS man that Stefan had ever met seemed to exclusively speak in Nazi platitudes and prayers to the great Messiah Adolf Hitler. It was odd and creepy. It reminded Stefan too much of the crazy people from his mother's church who couldn't get through a sentence without mentioning Jesus and His Great Sacrifice for Our Sins.

"Hopefully, he got a lot of great gifts," Stefan said, gesturing back towards the SA barrack. "We sent some chocolates and a note. Earlier, we bumped into this crazy lady who sent him a fucking cradle. Whoever unwraps the

Führer's presents for him is gonna have a laugh at that one."

"A cradle?" Stefan was grateful when that little anecdote seemed to make the SS man's mask fracture for a second as a genuine little chuckle ripped out of him. He must have realized he had faltered for a moment and seemed too human since he quickly cleared his throat and said, "A good gesture. Hopefully, the nation will be blessed enough to see many cradles filled with the Führer's children."

Stefan heard Axel repress something, either a laugh or possibly (and very understandably) a gag.

"Oh, where are my manners? Friedrich Dressler, SD Lieutenant." The Weasel, Dressler, gave a very slight bow and a viper-like smile. Armin let out another gruff little bark while Axel lifted a curious brow.

"SD?" Axel repeated. "You're one of Heydrich's men?"

Stefan hadn't known what Axel was talking about at the time—just because he was a Nazi didn't mean he bothered to read Nazi newspapers, after all. He would learn later that Heydrich was Reinhard Heydrich, certified asshole with one of the most punchable faces God had ever placed on a human. In the future, Heydrich would be Hitler's Hangman. Back then, in 1934, he had been Himmler's underling, the chief of the intelligence wing of the SS, the SD.

Dressler, Heydrich's little minion, chuckled. "Yes, indeed, and I'm very proud of it. He's a great man." (Stefan would later laugh as he remembered that particular part of the conversation since *nobody* in the SS thought that Heydrich was a great man. A useful man, sure. A scary man, certainly. A man who was really great at murder, most definitely. Great, though? Absolutely not.)

"Ah, sorry, I didn't get your names," Dressler said, waving for them to introduce themselves.

"Sergeant Axel Lahner," Axel said, flashing a charming smile at Heydrich's goon. He gave Armin's leash a slight tug when the dog decided that Dressler was getting a bit too close and lunged forward, snapping at the SD officer's jackboots. Dressler's eyes glistened.

"Lahner as in Paul Lahner? The philanthropist?"

"That would be my father," Axel said, caution giving way to the affectionate pride that he always displayed when he spoke of his father. Stefan saw Dressler's posture loosen a little, as though hearing of Axel's lineage was relaxing.

"Good breeding you have," the SS man said. "Paul Lahner is a true friend to the Party."

"I'm sure Herr Lahner sent Hitler a present that's worth his time," Stefan joked. "Something better than a cradle."

Again, Dressler's mask slipped a bit as he chuckled. He turned to Stefan, nodding, an invitation for Stefan to introduce himself.

"Stefan Harkel, gutter trash."

Stefan's self-deprecating introduction elicited another genuine half-laugh from the SS man. "Now, now, every German has value, even if they aren't from old money," Dressler said. "After all, our dearest Führer is the son of a mere civil servant."

"True, but Axel here has more *literal* value," Stefan quipped, deadpan, barely repressing the urge to projectile vomit all over Dressler. The SS man was probably about five seconds away from serenading them about how humble little Adolf was born in a manger under a rainbow or some shit.

"You gentlemen live here with Vogel?" Dressler asked.

"Nah ah," Stefan said. Lying to the SD officer would almost certainly be a bad idea, but saying that he and Axel were "roommates" would be too obvious given the reputation of the SA. Stefan settled for a half-lie. "We're neighbors. Barracks are too rowdy. No privacy."

"*Neighbors*" wasn't quite a lie. They slept next to one another, so technically they were bed-neighbors. Dressler's shoulders relaxed even more, and Stefan almost chuckled. The SS man no doubt thought that he was in decent company: two men who had seen the homoerotic rowdiness of Vogel's barracks and left in disgust. Fellow homophobes.

"I see. Understandable, if the rumors I've heard about that queer Vogel are to be believed. I've heard he sometimes brings children as young as twelve…"

"That's not Wilhelm!" snapped Stefan, his neutral expression morphing into a scowl. "That's total bullshit! Wilhelm's a good—!"

"Stefan, Stefan," Axel said, shoving Armin's leash into his boyfriend's arms, likely to stop him from outright decking Dressler in his smug weasel face. Axel flashed the sort of smile that made Stefan want to kiss him, SD officer be damned, and said, "Wilhelm's like a father to him; he gets protective. Being honest, we obviously don't condone Troop-Leader Vogel's degeneracy, but he *is* a very good man. Sick in the head, of course, but not *that* sick."

"Slippery slope," Dressler argued, taking out another cigarette and lighting up. Axel shook his head.

"I disagree," he said. "There's no need to associate one form of degeneracy with another. Not every pedophile is also incestuous. And of course, some forms of degeneracy are more harmful than others. Wilhelm, I think, really does believe what he writes about a positive, masculine form of homosexuality. The Roman sort, you know, that's what he's envisioned. He's religious about not harming anyone, though, I can tell you that much. And of course, he's utterly devoted to the Führer and the Cause."

"Hm." Dressler took a draw from his cigarette, inhaled, and blew smoke in the direction of Vogel's barracks. "Agree to disagree for now. I'll trust that if you uncover anything that contradicts your assumptions, you'll report it to the SS."

"Of course," Axel said with a nod. "I know we're a bit biased since Wilhelm is our friend, but the nation and the Cause will always come first."

"Always," Dressler confirmed, his eyes flitting towards Stefan.

"Yeah," Stefan muttered, bobbing his head. "We should get going. Dog's antsy."

"Wouldn't want to stress him!" chuckled Dressler, grinning at the growling mutt. He extended a hand towards Axel, who shook it firmly.

"You gentlemen seem very discerning," Dressler noted, smiling at Stefan even as he shook Axel's hand. "If you ever feel like switching to the SS, come down to our headquarters and I can help. The pay is better, and the reputation is…cleaner."

"We'll be sure to think about it!" chirped Axel. They bade farewell to Dressler and then hurried back to their apartment, only daring to enter together once they were certain that they hadn't been followed.

Stefan, not wanting dirty little Armin to ruin their furniture, dragged the mutt to the bathroom and washed him in the tub while Axel leaned against the bathroom door, smiling as he watched his boyfriend struggle to keep the slippery hound from leaping out of the sudsy water.

"'Cleaner reputation,' bah!" Stefan scoffed, scrubbing Armin behind the ears. "I dunno much about the SS, but I know their reputation ain't clean!"

"About as clean as Armin is on a daily basis," Axel quipped. "You know, my parents have been wanting me to join the SS."

"Seriously?" Stefan laughed, nearly getting soap in his eyes as Armin tried to escape the tub.

"Carries more prestige," Axel said casually, adding with a coy little purr, "And I would look good in the uniform."

"I'm not boosting your ego by responding to that," teased Stefan. "Your ego's big enough."

"*Mean.*"

"What'd you say to your folks?"

"'I'll think about it.'"

"Which means 'no.'"

"Same response I give whenever they ask me to go see a matchmaker."

"Exactly. 'No.'"

"Well, on the bright side, they're so hung up on me joining the SS that they've stopped constantly pressuring me to find a woman."

"Small miracles. Towel!"

Axel ran to retrieve a towel as Stefan drained the tub and hastened to dry the dog. Armin did his best to dry *himself* off by shaking vigorously, sending sudsy water into Stefan's eyes, but he still needed to be toweled off before his masters would let him out of the bathroom.

As soon as Armin was dried and subsequently freed, he ran into the living room, hopped onto the couch, and started rolling about, kicking his legs into the air, and rubbing his back against the cushions.

"I *just* dried you, boy! Good God!" laughed Stefan. Axel gave him a towel for his own face, which Stefan accepted happily.

"You, uh…" Stefan muttered once he was certain that his hair was dry, idly fiddling with the soaked towel in his hands. "You don't think that Dressler fellow's going to arrest Wilhelm, do you?"

"I don't know," said Axel, ever earnest, taking the towel from Stefan's hands and chucking it into the bathtub. "There isn't much we can do about that sort of thing except warn him to be on guard."

"Right. We'll do that tomorrow. For now..."

Stefan grabbed Axel by the collar and dragged him into a long kiss, then pushed him into their bedroom and slammed the door shut. They enjoyed the rest of their night, and the next day, they made sure to tell Wilhelm about Dressler.

The Troop Leader laughed off their concerns. "Don't you worry about it," Wilhelm said. "Those little boys in the SS don't have any real guts."

He was wrong.

———————— ▽ ————————

The Night of Long Knives was not a single night. That was to be expected, of course. Stefan would not learn the intricate details until much later, but brilliant, devious Reinhard Heydrich and his equally devious but not quite as brilliant co-conspirators, Heinrich Himmler and Hermann Goering, had planned to eliminate the SA for quite some time.

It most certainly didn't take a single night for Adolf Hitler to turn against his old friend Ernst Röhm, one of the only people he had ever allowed to call him by his first name. But Heydrich was a slippery little eel, Himmler was a plague-ridden rat that didn't look nearly as threatening as he truly was, and Goering was as charming as he was obese. For a long while, they had all fanned the flames of Hitler's paranoia, telling him that Röhm wanted to overthrow him.

Ernst Röhm didn't make things any better, running around and calling Hitler a reactionary, a swine, saying that Hitler couldn't walk all over him and his massive Brownshirt army.

But Hitler *could* walk all over him and his gigantic gang of rowdy street fighters. For some time he didn't, perhaps out of loyalty. But circumstances changed. Hitler was no longer a revolutionary. He was Chancellor, and when old man Hindenburg kicked the bucket, he intended to be more than that. A true national leader, an all-powerful Führer.

But Hitler wouldn't get far without the support of the German upper-class. The conservatives of the regular army who hated queer, loud, violent Ernst Röhm and his men.

Loyalty couldn't overwhelm Hitler's lust for power, and Heydrich, Himmler, and Goering saw to it that he could order a purge of the Brownshirts with righteous self-assurance. *I was protecting myself,* he could say. *They were plotting against me.*

And so, on the last day of June in 1934, the purge began. All across Germany, men were executed in the streets or hauled to concentration camps by the SS that would ultimately replace the SA as Hitler's ideological army. Ernst Röhm was yanked out of bed and dragged to a jail cell. *All revolutions eat their own children,* he would scoff that night, and the next night, he would be shot.

All throughout those bloody nights, it was Reinhard Heydrich running the police, giving calls, making death lists, and ruthlessly berating anyone who wanted to show their SA comrades an ounce of mercy. *Traitors like them deserve no mercy.*

It was Reinhard Heydrich, ultimately, who gave the order to wipe out Wilhelm Vogel's troop. Friedrich Dressler's report had made it clear that they all needed to die. The little family of Stormtroopers was too tight-knit. Happily, Heydrich rubber-stamped their deaths, but Friedrich Dressler had left two names off of the list he submitted to the Blond Beast. Stefan Harkel and Axel Lahner, who didn't live in Wilhelm's barracks, were passed over by the Young God of Death.

The Nazi anthem, the *Horst-Wessel Lied*, had a lyric that Wilhelm had always been fond of: "Sharpen long knives on the sidewalk. When the hour comes, we'll be ready for the slaughter."

Wilhelm wasn't ready when the hour came and the first Night of Long Knives began, and it was the first night that Stefan remembered. The rest of the purge was a blur, but he remembered waking up to take Armin for a late-night bathroom break after the poor dog climbed into his and Axel's bed, whining.

Armin was a picky pooper, and so Stefan didn't think much of it when the mutt ended up dragging him away from his and Axel's complex. Wilhelm's barracks were only a few blocks away from their apartment, and Armin's favorite toilet spot was the stretch of grass right in front of the SA building, so Stefan sleepily allowed himself to be pulled along.

He only snagged a brief glance at the barracks as he rounded the corner with Armin. A brief glance was all he needed, though; the windows were broken, the building was swarming with SS men, and Friedrich Dressler was standing over a line of corpses neatly filed along the street.

Stefan didn't need to get a close look to be able to tell from the sheer number of corpses that every member of Wilhelm Vogel's troop had been murdered. Not wanting to join them, he grabbed his dog and ducked behind the wall, perking up his ears and picking up the final snippets of an argument between Dressler and a few policemen.

"...so just file it away as a self-defense," Dressler commanded curtly. "I don't have time to appear in court."

"Errr...sir...Vogel was shot in the head."

"Yeah, exactly, I shot him because he resisted arrest and attacked me."

"He was shot in the *back* of the head."

"Back, front, what's the difference?! His head's got a hole in it either way, and he isn't getting an autopsy!"

"It just looks a little...clean."

"Clean, ha! Doesn't look clean to me! Tell anyone who asks that I'm a really damn good shot! I don't have time for this! I have to call Heydrich!"

Stefan didn't hear anything else Dressler said over the frantic pounding of his own heartbeat. It was pure instinct that drove him to run all the way back to his apartment with Armin in his arms. He crashed into his and Axel's apartment, dropped the poor mutt, and locked the door behind him.

Axel heard the commotion and shuffled out of their room, silver eyes weary and anxious. One didn't live this long in a turbulent nation and merely dismiss the frantic slamming of a front door.

"Stefan...?" he said. Stefan rushed towards Axel, who immediately wrapped the trembling shorter man into a tight embrace.

"What happened?" Axel asked, worry dripping from every syllable. Stefan would, in the future, be embarrassed by how he acted right then as he tried to explain what he'd seen. How he buried his face into Axel's shoulder and sobbed like a hysterical child. How he barely managed to declare that every member of their Brownshirt family was dead, murdered not by the evil Jews or the vile communists, but by the Cause they had loyally served.

Stefan felt Armin pawing at his shoes, felt Axel tremble

even as he patted his boyfriend's back and begged him to stop crying.

"Stefan, we're all right," Axel whispered. "We're fine…it's going to be alright…"

He was wrong.

Chapter NINE

1943

While One-Twenty dug a shallow grave behind the rotting little shack, Stefan sat in the decrepit rocking chair. For a very long time, he simply stared at the four little words that formed the name of the man who had ruined his life.

Stefan had never entertained the idea that he would ever receive the soul of someone that had affected him so directly, so personally. He had certainly never thought that a minor Master like himself would ever own the soul of the Butcher of Prague.

If he had ever pondered the idea, he would have assumed that if he was handed such a Contract, he would dive right in and immediately begin skinning Reinhard Heydrich with a rusty spoon or crucifying him on a cactus, and while Stefan would almost certainly be doing those things, right then he felt oddly numb. Maybe because holding Heydrich's immortal soul was bringing back memories that he had tried his best to stop caring about for the sake of his own sanity. A part of him didn't even want to go into Zone N-1 at all.

He had to, though. If not to torture Heydrich, then at least to find out a little more about what Alice had tried to tell him about this "Grandmaster."

So eventually, Stefan shut his eyes and thought: *I want to go to Zone N-1.*

Again, he was met with the familiar sensation of falling, that Axel-driving-through-the-countryside feeling. This time, it was much more intense, like he was falling into a much deeper hole. Maybe he was. He had never considered the fact that more important Zones holding bigger shitheads might be different, that the Master of Reinhard Heydrich was more important in the eyes of Ha-Satan than the Master of Hans Hansmann the Random Nazi Asshole.

Heydrich would probably be weirdly delighted if he ever found that out, though, so Stefan certainly wouldn't be telling him.

Stefan landed upon a silver throne, though this one seemed larger than the one in Zone N-74. When he glanced about the Master Room, he found that its layout was exactly like that of N-74's save for the fact that the throne and the space itself seemed slightly bigger.

The only true difference was one that Stefan noticed when he hopped off the grand seat and turned to look at the wall behind him. The crimson letters that hung above the silver throne were similar but had seemingly been edited with what Stefan hoped was merely red paint.

Here Sits

the

God of

~~Zone N-1~~

Nazi-Land

"Nazi-Land?" he muttered. Realization dawned on him, and he grimaced, glancing at the wall of Masters. This wall was also slightly different: his portrait was up but branded "Master 4." Three other portraits hung before his. He barely glanced at the first two Masters and instead gazed upon the third: a young, pretty girl with soft blue eyes, pretty blonde hair tied into two braids, and a neutral expression.

"*Alice*. Got it." Stefan sighed, staring at his predecessor's picture. "Quite a rabbit hole you fell down, sweetie…"

Stefan slowly turned away from the four portraits and started down the hall. He lingered by the triangle-decorated door for a moment. Even though he was, within the Zone, little more than a soul that looked like flesh-and-blood, Stefan nevertheless felt his heart absolutely pounding as he reached for the handle.

"Here it goes," Stefan said, and he stepped into Reinhard Heydrich's little corner of Hell.

Stefan shut the door behind him and found himself standing in a sprawling office. A chandelier that must have cost at least a barrel of gold teeth shimmered on the ceiling. A dead fern rested above a fine marble mantelpiece, its brown leaves falling onto the ornate carpet. A huge gold-and-black banner of an eagle clutching a swastika hung above a giant oaken desk.

And behind that giant desk was a giant man. Reinhard Heydrich was well over six feet tall with light blond hair and blue eyes that looked like a chunk of frozen ocean water. The tall SS man appeared to be the perfect Aryan, a standout among the decidedly racially imperfect members of the Nazi hierarchy. (*A true Nazi*, Papa Fox had once joked, *should be blond like Hitler, tall like Goebbels, and slim like Goering.*)

Heydrich lifted those frozen-ocean eyes of his and

regarded his new Master with what could only be described as annoyance. "Ah," he said. "Another new one."

Stefan had never heard Heydrich's voice before, and so when his new Subject spoke, he nearly started laughing his ass off. He had expected either a resonating Hitlerian boom or maybe a hiss like a snake, but instead, Heydrich's voice was more akin to the bleat of a goat: oddly high-pitched, like that of a boy that had not quite finished puberty yet. Stefan supposed that explained why Papa Fox had always called him "Billy-Goat Heydrich."

Heydrich must have seen Stefan's lips quirk upwards in amusement because his icy blue eyes flashed with anger, and it seemed like he wanted nothing more than to lunge at the undesirable before him. The Hangman seemed to quickly remember himself, however, as he sighed heavily and stood up, back straight, eyes narrowed, the posture of a beaten dog that knew better than to snap but hadn't quite been utterly broken yet.

"So, what exactly are you supposed to be, Master Four?" he queried, and Stefan grunted. Fantastic, another number to remember. First, he'd had to memorize his serial codes at Dachau, then he'd trained himself to answer to Black Fox Five, now he would have to balance being Master One of Zone N-74 and Master Four of Zone N-1. It would be much easier if he could just be Stefan again.

"What?" Stefan repeated. It was a bit strange: he was the God of this place and this soul, the new God of Nazi-Land, and yet for a moment, he almost forgot the power emanating from the triangular piece of paper attached to his heart. It almost felt like he and Heydrich were on equal footing, especially when the Blond Beast gave an ugly, smug-as-fuck sneer and held up one finger.

"Master One was a Jew," Heydrich said.

The Hangman ticked off another finger. "Master Two was gypsy filth."

Three fingers, and with particular vitriol. "And Master Three was a worthless Czech."

"Alice, you mean, that little girl," growled Stefan, taking a step forward. That alone, one step, was usually enough to make his own Subjects whimper and cower and apologize for their impertinence. He saw the barest hint of fear in Heydrich's eyes. Nevertheless, the Hangman refused to move.

"Alice," Heydrich drawled, and his little smirk stretched. "Ah, that was her name? That explains quite a bit. Explains why she used to call this place Nazi-Land. She fancied herself very creative. I guess she *was* creative. She's dead?"

Stefan nodded once. Heydrich grinned.

"I hope she suffered."

That did it. A few words was all it took for Stefan to wipe that ugly smile off the Blond Beast's face. "Reinhard Heydrich's left leg rotted away painfully and slowly. It burned and felt like utter and complete agony."

And so it was. Heydrich collapsed to the carpeted floor as an unholy smell filled the office, and while Stefan couldn't see the result of his divine decree through Heydrich's puffy uniform pants, it must have been a gory sight.

"Fuck you, you sadistic Jew piece of shit!" Heydrich snarled, trying and failing to hold in tears of agony.

"I'm not a Jew," Stefan said, crossing the room. He sat on Heydrich's desk, smirking down at the kneeling, helpless dead man. "And you're one to call other people sadists, especially given what you just said about that little girl."

"'Little girl', *ha!* As though she's so innocent! *She's* the real sadist. You didn't see what she did while she was Master!" Heydrich hissed.

"I'm sure whatever she did, you deserved much worse," Stefan growled, idly glancing down at the death-warrants laying on Heydrich's desk.

"I didn't even do anything to her!" Heydrich insisted, evidently getting used to the abundant pain quickly as sat up a bit, drew in a deep breath, and refused to show anything more than a grimace. "We were good to her, the damn little ingrate!"

"She told you about herself, then? Enlighten me," Stefan said. Heydrich hesitated for a moment, scrutinizing Stefan's features and clearly trying to discern whether or not refusing to answer would lead to a Command.

He must have correctly guessed that it would because he huffed in resignation.

"According to her," Heydrich said, "she was from a small Czech village. Evidently, they had some connection to the Slav bastards who killed me, and so Hitler ordered the entire village to be destroyed. Shot all the men…she said he even diverted the rivers and destroyed the roads, but I'm sure she was lying."

"She wasn't," Stefan confirmed. The Nazis didn't often like to broadcast their massacres, but the obliteration of the Czech village of Lidice had been the one exception. The Nazi press had bragged about completely destroying that village in retaliation for Heydrich's assassination, killing all Lidice's men and shipping all of its women and children to concentration camps.

"She blamed *me* for all of that even though I had nothing to do with it!" Heydrich exclaimed, earning a derisive snort from the God of Nazi-Land.

"Nothing at all?" Stefan said, and the Hangman huffed.

"I don't see how getting assassinated by someone who happened to be from that village is *my* fault!"

"You asked for it."

"I was good to the Czechs! Better than they deserved! I could have turned Czechoslovakia into Poland and utterly decimated the rabble! Bormann wanted to, but I was willing to pull the wheat from the chaff! Take time, allow those with good race and attitude to thrive. I even gave some leeway to those with bad race and a good attitude."

"Anyone willing to be enslaved, in other words."

"Anyone who accepted the scientific *fact* of the racial hierarchy. I could have starved them all, had them all shot! Instead, I gave their workers raises, gave them security, gave them food, let them have cultural festivals!"

"Bread and circuses," Stefan scoffed, tipping over an inkwell and watching the black ink flow across the desk, consuming the death warrants. "You didn't do that for their benefit, you did it to keep them docile. So you could eventually sort out the wheat from the chaff without any trouble."

"Does that matter?"

"It certainly didn't matter to Alice once her family was murdered."

"*Executed.*"

"You fucking people…" laughed Stefan bitterly, shaking his head.

"And her family might have been complacent in *my* murder!" Heydrich argued, earning a vicious laugh from his Master.

"Probably weren't, and if they were, they should'a gotten a medal, not a bullet."

"But nonetheless, even then, we National Socialists were willing to show mercy to those in Lidice with potential! The SS didn't just mow everyone down! They spared children with good racial characteristics and sent them to the Reich to be adopted out. That isn't the sort of thing they did centuries ago."

"Very lovely that you hold yourself to the high standards of the Dark Ages."

"*Fine.* The Judeo-Bolsheviks you work with wouldn't do such a thing. One member of a family conspires against Stalin, he wipes *everyone* out and shows *no* mercy."

"'I'm occasionally not as evil as Stalin' isn't the great defense you think it is. Did you try to pull that one in front of the Court in Heaven? No wonder your attorney lost."

"I didn't even have anything to do with that Czech village. I was a bit busy *being dead!*" Heydrich demurred aggressively. "I'm merely trying to illustrate that Master Three was unnecessarily cruel and vengeful when we were extremely merciful. She at least looked racially promising, and so she wasn't deported with the rest of the rabble. She went off to live with a German family in the Reich. We were willing to give her a good future!"

"A good future being a brainwashed little Nazi, serving the people who killed her real parents," snapped Stefan, anger bubbling in his chest. He knew that the SS hadn't killed *every* child in Lidice. Some of them, those like Alice who had blonde hair and blue eyes, had been kidnapped. Sent to the Reich to be "reprogrammed." His admiration for Alice's strength reached new heights. He normally hated kids, but it was clear that little Alice had been forced to grow up fast.

"She made her choice," Heydrich spat. "She refused to learn, refused to speak German, refused to salute the Führer, and so she was deported. The last time she came down here, she mentioned that she was on a train heading East. I can only hope that she got what she deserved."

"You really think you're a good person, don't you?" Stefan muttered, and he wasn't entirely sure why he was surprised. All Nazis, he supposed, twisted their brains into pretzels to make themselves into the righteous victims. Somehow or another, the *Einsatzgruppen* officer who shot Jewish toddlers convinced himself that those toddlers were out to get him.

Surprisingly, though, Heydrich didn't immediately answer in the affirmative. He squirmed, looked down at his rotted leg, winced, then muttered, "I have honor. That's what counts."

"Ha! *Honor!* Sure! You're just *honorably* serving an amazing child-killing Cause."

"That isn't what the Cause is about," Heydrich snapped, turning his face away from the God of Nazi-Land and focusing on the dead fern above the mantle.

"It's definitely a major feature," Stefan sneered.

"That's *not* what it's about, you wouldn't understand…"

"I wouldn't understand the great National Socialist Cause to strengthen Germany and reclaim the land stolen under Versailles. This ultimate goal must be served by requisitioning *Lebensraum* from traditionally German lands and from those ruled by races too stupid to truly utilize it. The German nation is like a man who cannot be healthy until he stretches out his limbs, and cramped urban conditions have allowed Jews to unleash degeneracy unto our populace."

Even Stefan was a little surprised by the ease with which he was still able to vomit up that Nazi garbage. Axel *had* kept elbowing him in the gut whenever he'd zone out during ideological conferences and lessons, though, so SA Private Stefan Harkel hadn't been utterly clueless about the Cause he was serving.

Heydrich's eyes widened, an odd look for him. His eyes always seemed narrowed, either in suspicion or disdain or hatred, and genuine shock didn't suit his harsh features.

"I know all the bullshit," Stefan said. "Troop-Leader Wilhelm Vogel taught us well. He was loyal."

"Ah...so that's it." Wide eyes narrowed again, and Heydrich's lips curled. "A degenerate Brownshirt who escaped the purges. So, you're upset I killed Röhm and Vogel, that's it? Did I kill your boyfriend, you *faggot?*"

Stefan might have admired Heydrich for the sheer gall he had, provoking a God the way he did.

Instead, he just said, "Reinhard Heydrich was lit on fire, a fire that burned and hurt but didn't destroy and couldn't be put out."

Stefan didn't like to set people on fire most of the time. The smell was bad, and he had passed through enough villages visited by Viktor Naden to gain a healthy distaste for the sight of burned corpses. He had learned, therefore, to make his immolation orders specific, and he did so right then. Reinhard Heydrich was lit ablaze and filled all of the false Prague with his screams, but while the fire burned just as hot as any other, he didn't perish.

All Heydrich could do was scream and scream, and that was good, because he deserved it. Stefan watched the man that had ruined his life scream his lungs sore and felt indescribably powerful and *good…*

"Five! *Five!*"

And then he was back on Earth. Stefan almost cursed. He'd been too busy, too distracted by the God-like feeling that tormenting the Man with the Iron Heart gave him. He'd forgotten his real mission and hadn't gotten a chance to ask Heydrich about the Grandmaster.

Too late now. They needed to get moving, get as far away from the nearby camp as possible.

"I buried her already, the girl," One-Twenty said. "I was going to say Kaddish for her..."

"Don't," Stefan interrupted, hopping off the rocking chair and grabbing his bag. "She wasn't a Jew."

The Russian's brow crinkled. "I thought you said you didn't know…"

"My brain's a bit on the fritz 'cause a little kid just died next to me, all right?" snapped Stefan. One-Twenty winced and gave him a look that was way too much like the one Gerhard had given their father when he'd been yelled at for some minor sin. Stefan immediately felt like an absolute piece of shit.

"Sorry, kid," he sighed, patting the Russian's shoulder. "I…I'm sorry."

"It's fine, I'm not delicate," One-Twenty assured his commander. "I'm just worried about you. Seeing things like that too often, it'll get to anyone. Even One needs breaks on occasion."

"*Breaks* for her involve breaking Nazi necks most of the time," quipped Stefan, earning a smile and a chuckle from his comrade.

"True enough. We should get moving or we might miss more survivors or escapees. The child didn't mention anything about friends, did she?"

"No, just that the Kommandant was after her, which means he'll probably be coming this way soon to look for her. We've gotta move. Get back to the Bunker, then contact Papa Fox."

Papa Fox would certainly want to hear about Stefan's newest Contract. Maybe he would ask for Heydrich's soul himself.

"All right," One-Twenty said, checking his rifle. "Then let's put the cache away and…

BAM!

"*Gevalt!*"

"Gevalt" was likely some sort of Yiddish curse, the sort of thing Torah-toting Jewish boys like One-Twenty were never supposed to say. Whatever it meant, though, it was more than warranted as all of a sudden, bullets began to fly through the holes in Base Twelve's walls.

Quickly, both Black Foxes hit the floor and crawled towards the gaps in the building. A cursory peek outside revealed that a small battalion of SS men were ducking behind the evergreen trees. Stefan was not the best shot in the world, and he was already dizzy after the long day he'd had, so when he exchanged fire, he didn't manage to hit anyone.

One-Twenty, who was typically a better shot than Stefan, might have managed to hit one Nazi if a bullet hadn't torn through the cheap wooden structure, nearly topping the entire building, and embedded itself in the Russian's leg.

"Shit!" hissed Stefan, knowing full well that a bullet wound to the leg could be fatal if not treated right away. He had learned not to dismiss such injuries when doing so early in his Black Fox career had cost him one of his comrades. He dropped his gun, tore a part of his coat into a strip, and tied it around the wound while the Russian hissed in pain and begged him to keep shooting the fascists.

"Not if you're gonna bleed to death," Stefan said. Once the tourniquet was tied, he moved to grab his weapon again only to be greeted by a gun barrel poking through one huge hole in the wall, aimed right at his face.

"Hands up, now!" the Nazi commanded.

"Fuck you," snapped Stefan, but at risk of getting his skull blown off and seeing One-Twenty carted off to the camp alone, he obeyed.

The little shack was immediately swarmed by SS men. One-Twenty, fortunately, had lost his cyanide pill long ago, and Stefan had dumped his early on since he was confident in his ability to escape Nazis through means other than suicide. The two Black Foxes surrendered with more aggravation than fear, for both of them had survived being captured by the SS before.

But then, the SS soldiers stepped aside, and their commanding officer marched into the little house.

"Well, well, well...Stefan. I was wondering when I'd see you again."

Stefan felt his heart roil as he beheld a smirking man in a pristine SS uniform marred only by a Contract that rested right beneath a bronze SS pin.

Stefan's jaw tightened, and he scowled up at the man.

"Axel," he said, and his ex-boyfriend chuckled fondly.

"That's Kommandant Lahner to you."

—————— ▽ ——————

Chapter
TEN

1934

He had loved Axel, even though Axel was arrogant.

He had loved Axel, even though Axel was a coward who always wanted so desperately to fit in with the crowd, with the masses, no matter how stupid they were.

He had loved Axel, even though Axel thought that life was a series of bargains and tradeoffs.

He had loved Axel, even though he was sometimes convinced that Axel hated him as much as he loved him—no, *because* he loved him. Because Axel's life would have been much simpler if he could have just had his lavender marriage and kept quiet about his real desires for the rest of his days, but Stefan had complicated things like he always did. Ruined perfect plans.

He had loved Axel. He was sure that he still loved him, actually, even though Axel was a child-murderer. Because love was exactly what Stefan had feared it would be: a vicious parasite that pretended to be a welcome guest. A parasite that wouldn't let go of its host even when everything went to Hell.

And everything did go to Hell soon after the Night of Long Knives. Stefan would never quite remember what happened in the two weeks between sobbing in Axel's arms after Wilhelm was murdered and The Breakup.

The Breakup, as Stefan called it, capitalized like the historical tragedy it was, like The Eruption of Vesuvius or The Sinking of the Titanic or The Day Hitler Was Born. It happened because Axel came home one day wearing the uniform of the men who had murdered Wilhelm Vogel.

"What the fuck is that?" Stefan asked while Axel, smiling as though nothing was wrong, as though he wasn't wearing death's shadow, knelt down and warmly greeted Armin.

"We're all right, just like I said," the newly minted SS man said, looking up with a smile that withered when he saw the expression on his lover's face. Axel heaved a deep sigh and stood up.

Armin, sensing the tension, skittered between the men, grabbing various toys and flinging them at his masters' feet in an attempt to distract them with play. Stefan would have truly liked nothing more than to grab a rope and play tug-of-war with Armin, to pretend like all of this was just fine.

But it wasn't fine, and so he scowled like he did whenever Axel did something that demanded an explanation.

"Look, if you don't want to be eaten by wolves, it's best to join the pack," Axel sighed. "I spoke to Dressler."

"That weaselly fucker from the other day? Heydrich's guy?" exclaimed Stefan. "The shithead who *murdered* Wilhelm?!"

"Stefan..." Axel stepped forward, too close in that

disgusting uniform that summoned memories of seeing his friends' corpses. Stefan leapt back.

"Do not—!" he cried. Axel winced but obeyed, dropping his hand and giving his beau a foot of breathing room.

"Stefan, listen to me," Axel said, his tone remaining gentle but now with a firm edge, like he was speaking to a small, stupid child. "This is what's best for us. The SS is the elite of the elite. I'm in now. I'm going to be working with Dressler personally. And with my father's connections, it won't be long until I'm high up in the Party. I'll be above reproach. We won't have to worry about anything ever again. We'll live like kings, you and I."

"I'd rather fucking die than put on that uniform!" Stefan said, wrapping his arms about himself and squeezing tight. Armin barked and tried to jump on him, but he stepped away from Armin, who finally realized that there was nothing he could do to salvage this situation and retreated under the dining room table with a soft whimper.

"You don't have to," Axel argued, pressing a hand to his chest. "I can take care of everything…"

"How could you even *think* of doing this? The SS killed our friends, *my* friends! The people we loved, the people who were loyal to the Party, they killed them!"

"I know that, Stefan. It's not as though I approve of that, but…well, what's done is done. Bristling and snarling and, what, plotting revenge? That won't do us any good. We have to move forward just like the Party is moving forward."

"Moving…moving forward?" sputtered Stefan. "You call killing our friends moving forward?!"

"Stefan, you're being too emotional…"

"Of fucking course I'm being emotional, Axel! You're working for the bastard who killed Wilhelm!"

"Wilhelm was my friend too. I loved him, but…"

"Oh! Oooh, you *loved* him!" Stefan exclaimed, half laughing, half screaming. "This is how you treat people you *love*, hm? You shrug and say, 'Fuck it, better get in bed with the people who killed him!'"

"Stefan…"

"What if *I* was in Wilhelm's barracks that night, hm? You 'love' me after all! Would you still be joining the SS?"

"Stefan!"

"You *would*, wouldn't you?" Stefan realized, gaping in horror as Axel curled and uncurled his black-gloved fists and avoided his lover's accusatory gaze. "I would have been in the barracks that night if you hadn't asked me to come live with you. I would have *died*."

"But you weren't there, and you didn't die," Axel whispered, bowing his head. The visor of the skull-emblazoned SS cap cast a shadow on his face that obscured his grimace.

"But what if I was?" Stefan pressed, and Axel squirmed.

"You *weren't*…"

"Answer the damn question! If I'd died, if the SS had killed me, would you still join them?"

Axel didn't answer, which was itself an answer. Stefan hated himself for ever letting his guard down. Love was conditional, like Axel had said, and Stefan Harkel always found a way to lose it.

"So, you don't love me," Stefan declared, and he tried to sound strong even though a sob was absolutely clawing at the inside of his throat. Axel looked up, silver eyes shimmering with what could only be described as fearful agitation.

"I do love you, Stefan, I love you!" he insisted. "I don't love how you're trying to control my choices, especially when I'm doing this for both of us! Like it or not, the SA was a liability…"

"A *liability*?!"

"They were loud, rowdy street fighters!" Axel argued, gesturing to a swastika flag that hung above their fireplace. Stefan had wanted to tear that flag down after the Night of Long Knives, but Axel had insisted on leaving it up. "We're trying to build a government!"

"You mean Hitler's simpering up to that windbag Hindenburg, trying to get a few scraps of power before he croaks! Trying to appeal to the conservatives in the army!"

"*Yes*, Stefan!" Axel cried, throwing up his hands, anxiety giving way to utter frustration. "He *had* to do it! That doesn't mean it was good, but if you think of it from his perspective, it clearly *had* to be done! I'm sorry, but the SA had a reputation for being a bunch of…"

"Degenerate rowdy homosexuals? A bunch of people *like me*, right?"

"Well, yes! That was always Wilhelm's problem! He was always so loud about it! Publishing papers about how it should be *acceptable* in a fascist society to be a homosexual! He was just *begging* to be purged! I cared about him, but he was a fool and—!"

Slap!

Stefan had never slapped any of his lovers before because Stefan was not an abusive piece of shit.

So when he did so right then, his hand connecting with Axel's cheek, making the fresh SS man wince more from the shock than the pain, Stefan knew that he had to leave. For both his sake and Axel's. He couldn't stay, couldn't see him in that uniform, couldn't hear him say such awful things. Not without becoming something that he didn't want to become.

So he avoided Axel's wide-eyed gaze. He didn't look at

poor, confused little Armin who was whimpering under the table. He just grabbed his wallet and ran for the door.

"Stefan, please…please understand," begged Axel as Stefan's hand brushed against the doorknob, and his lovely voice was as pained and pathetic as Arvin's cries on the day Stefan had been kicked out of his first home. Stefan might have stayed if Axel hadn't kept running his mouth. "The SS is the future of Germany, of the Party!""

Stefan gripped the doorknob tight. "If those bastards are the future of the Party, I don't want anything to do with it. And if they're *your* future, I don't want anything to do with *you*!"

"Stefan!" cried Axel, but Stefan was already racing out the door, blinded by anger and tears.

———— ▽ ————

Chapter
ELEVEN

Stefan was not surprised when he woke up in the nicest jail cell he'd ever been kept in. His head was spinning something awful since one of the guards had knocked him out after he'd lunged at a chuckling Axel Lahner, but otherwise he was unharmed.

"Good morning, darling."

Fuck, Stefan thought, sitting up on the plush bed he'd been dumped on. He wasn't handcuffed or chained up, so it might have been relatively easy to attack Axel right then as the Kommandant sat in a cozy chair, smoking one of those damned cigarettes, but it would probably be fruitless. Axel was well-fed and in good shape, and worse, he almost certainly had One-Twenty imprisoned nearby. Until Stefan knew where his comrade was and figured out a way to free him, he couldn't afford to be hasty.

That was going to be tough. Stefan Harkel and *not being hasty* just didn't go together.

"Don't fucking call me that," Stefan snapped with

none of the tender teasing he had offered when they'd been together. Axel chuckled, a cruel imitation of the lovely laugh he'd once possessed, and jabbed his cigarette into an ashtray.

"Ah, forgive me," he said. "Wouldn't want to offend your new beau, assuming he's awake. Walls are thin." Axel jabbed his thumb towards the left wall. Stefan didn't let his relief show on his face. One-Twenty was alive, and not only that, but he was close by.

"I didn't know you fancied Jews," Axel sneered. "And worse, *Slavic* Jews. He's awfully young for you too."

"He's not my *beau*, asshole, he's just a kid," Stefan snapped.

"Oh ho! That fire of yours, Stefan...I missed it. It's been...how many years? Three? Four?"

"Too few," hissed Stefan, and Axel hummed.

"I missed you too. Good to see you've been keeping busy. You're with the Black Foxes, hm?"

"I'm Five," said Stefan, because fuck this weird secret identity bullshit. It didn't even matter, and it wouldn't be worth the bother of Axel trying to find out even out of curiosity. The Kommandant's eyes glistened with the sort of genuine pride he had displayed when he'd taught Armin to roll over.

"High ranked. I'm not surprised. That's my Stefan."

"I'm not your Stefan, and I haven't been your Stefan for nine years."

"Yet you haven't found a new man. Haven't even made a pass at that handsome young Russian?" chuckled Axel before his nose wrinkled and he spat, "At least you still have some taste. I admit, the thought of a *Jew* laying a hand on you..."

"Firstly: I'm not your property. Secondly: I do not have any taste, you're the evidence of that. Thirdly: it's fucking laughable that you think you're above a Jew,"

Stefan declared. "If you weren't a coward and a hypocrite, you'd slap a pink triangle next to that Contract."

Axel chuckled, and this time it was the dangerous sort, almost a rumble, like a lion bracing to pounce. "Ah. Yes. Now we get to the interesting part. I believe you encountered a young lady who had something. Something that belongs to me."

"I don't know what..."

"Don't bother, Stefan. We found the Czech's body buried near the little safehouse where we captured you and your friend. And since *he* doesn't have any Contracts..."

"Maybe it disappeared when she died."

"Stefan..." Axel stood, slowly strolled up to his ex-boyfriend, and brought a hand to the shorter man's cheek. Stefan cursed his stupid sex-deprived self as he felt his body heat up. He hated the fact that he *so* wanted to lunge forward and grab Axel and kiss him and yank him down onto the bed even though he knew what he was.

Axel must have seen Stefan's cheeks flush red. He let out a victorious chuckle as he reached for Stefan's breast, easily peeling the Zone N-1 Contract off him, leaving the Contract to Zone N-74 stuck above Stefan's heart.

"The top Contracts always make their way to the top," Axel chirped. "I'm glad you have two. When this silliness is over, I can show you how these things really work."

"Yeah?" hissed Stefan, glancing at the golden triangle shimmering on his ex-boyfriend's breast. "How many have you got?"

"Oh, I stopped counting a long time ago. But I have the most, I know that much. Ah, there's our man."

Axel unfurled the N-1 Contract and grinned as he examined Reinhard Heydrich's silver name. Stefan grunted.

"If it were that easy to take it, you'd already have it,"

Stefan observed, and Axel chuckled, releasing the Contract. Immediately, the paper folded itself back into a triangle and flew to Stefan, landing safely above his heart.

"My smart Stefan," Axel crooned. "Nothing is ever that easy, unfortunately. The more it's worth, the more you have to fight for it."

Axel leaned a bit closer, and Stefan sidestepped him. "So that's it, then," Stefan snapped. "You have to do that little ritual thing. I'd have to cross out my own name."

"That's right." Axel stepped forward again, and again Stefan dodged him. This was beginning to feel like the old days, the good days, the days before Axel was a child-murderer, when Stefan was stupid and a Nazi and didn't have to care about all the babies that Hitler was going to kill.

"You already had a Contract when you became Kommandant," Stefan guessed. "When'd you get it?"

"1941. The position of Kommandant makes it much easier to find other Masters. Hundreds of thousands of people pass through here. Statistically, there will be a lot of Masters, especially since Satan favors giving Contracts to Jews. Nobody else has it in their religion that he's a trustworthy servant of God, after all."

"And you torture them until they agree to give you their Contract."

"Them, their family, whatever works."

"I'm shocked Satan would give a shithead like you even *one* Contract."

"Oh, much more. He gave me a top Zone," Axel tapped the Contract on his chest like he was Hermann Goering showing off his newest medal. "Zone H-1. The Zone for Hebrew sinners."

Stefan grunted. He supposed that made sense. Satan wasn't handing out Contracts to *good* people, he was awarding them to *hateful* people, *angry* people, people who would torture their Subjects mercilessly. A Czech girl that had her life torn from her was the perfect Master for Reinhard Heydrich. A Nazi SS officer was the perfect Master for a sinful Jew. He had so much practice tormenting innocent Jews and obeying the Devil already, after all. Torturing dead, evil Jews wouldn't faze him.

"I earned many Contracts from my own good work in my initial Zone," Axel bragged. "That's rare, you know. Apparently, Ha-Satan doesn't like giving the Top Masters too many minor Zones. Wants them to focus on their big targets. But you know I'm never satisfied."

"That's why she called you 'Grandmaster,'" Stefan observed.

"'She'? Ah! Little Alice! Poor, poor little Alice. Very bold, very stubborn, very stupid. If she'd just given Heydrich's Zone to me, she wouldn't have had to suffer so."

"So, getting Heydrich's soul was so important to you that you tortured a little girl to death, hm?" Stefan snarled before sneering in his best imitation of the Blond Beast: "What, is he your boyfriend?"

"Please, you're going to make me sick," grunted Axel, and to be fair, the mere idea of it was indeed vomit-inducing. "Heydrich was a bastard, but he was *our* bastard, and he was damn good at his work."

"Killing Jews, you mean."

"And undesirables. Enemies of the State in general. We're worse off having lost his talents and his knowledge."

"That's why you're losing the war, eh?" scoffed Stefan, and that again made the mask fracture as Axel pouted like he had before, whenever Stefan had refused to give him a compliment.

"We are *not* losing the war," the Kommandant insisted. "However, the war would be going much better with him back at the helm. *Himmlers Hirn heißt Heydrich.*"

Himmler's brain is called Heydrich, an old Nazi motto that was quite true and, sadly for the Reich, meant that the Head of the SS had been brain-dead for a year.

"I don't exactly see what your evil plan is here, Axel," Stefan confessed. "Even if you get this Contract off'a me, what then? Are you gonna walk right up to the Berghof: 'Pardon me, my Führer, but I happen to have Reinhard Heydrich's soul in an invisible triangle that's on my chest. Please don't euthanize me for being insane.'"

"I *could* do that. It needn't be invisible forever. If I renounce it, non-Masters will be able to see it."

"That would sort of defeat the purpose, wouldn't it? You can't renounce it and then take it back, I imagine. Besides, Hitler may be crazy, but he's not *that* crazy. He'd never sign it if you gave it to him. He'd have you hauled off before you could even..."

"*Hitler* wouldn't. *Himmler* on the other hand...well, you know he's always been eccentric."

Shit. He was. Heinrich Himmler was well known for being weird as shit, weirder than even the average Nazi. He sent entire divisions of SS men to go hunting for mystic treasure in Tibet. He had SS men sit around in circles and attempt to use their *collective energy* to force a suspect into confessing. He thought that he was the literal reincarnation of Henry the Fowler. He already believed in weirder shit than Contracts and Zones.

If Axel tried to tell Himmler about the Contracts, he would listen, enraptured. He wouldn't roll his eyes and dismiss it all as the delusions of a madman. He would listen, he would believe, and if given the opportunity to sign a Contract, he would.

And if Axel gave Himmler the Contract to Zone N-1...

Realization made Stefan's eyes widen, and Axel chuckled fondly.

"Now you get it," the Kommandant said. "Himmler gets his brain back, we all get Heydrich back, and I'll be in Himmler's confidence."

No, no, no, no! Stefan thought, and it was a real struggle to keep the fear he felt from showing on his face. The resistance, the Allies, the people of Europe had suffered so much to take Heydrich down. It had cost them an entire wing of the resistance and thousands of lives. Entire villages had been burned to the ground and destroyed. Hundreds of children like Alice had lost everything, and while some people in the Black Foxes still thought that the inevitable reprisals hadn't been worth the high cost, everyone had agreed that taking out Heydrich had been a great achievement, a crippling blow against the Reich.

But it would all be for nothing if Axel got his mitts on Zone N-1. Heydrich's well-deserved torments would end —Himmler would no doubt hesitate to Command his old comrade. Not only that, but all of Heydrich's knowledge, all of those murderous skills that the Nazis had lost when he'd been killed, would be reclaimed by the Reich. Heydrich would, for all intents and purposes, be brought back from the dead.

"And I'm standing in your way," Stefan said. "I'm the *only* thing standing in your way."

"You *are* very good at that."

"So, what are you waiting for? Shove a broomstick up my ass, I don't care. I don't give a shit what you do, I'm *not* giving you the Contract."

"Oh, Stefan, Stefan…" Again, Axel reached out, and since he'd walked Stefan into the wall that separated him from One-Twenty's room, there was nowhere for the Black Fox to run.

"You know I would never hurt you, Stefan," Axel whispered, soft, genuine. He gently grasped Stefan by the chin. Stefan hated him, he hated him, he wanted to kiss him, he *hated* him...

The gentle smile became twisted and cruel. Axel released Stefan's chin and pointed to one of his SS medals. "But I don't have to, do I? Hm, what do you think? Maybe I'll kill one of the Jew whelps. One for every day you refuse to hand over the Contract?"

Stefan stood taller, jaw set, eyes flaring.

"Every hour?"

The Black Fox squared his shoulders. Axel's eyes flitted to the wall.

"Or," the Kommandant said in a singsong tone, "maybe I'll just torture your little pet Jew until you break. You saw what we did to Alice, and I wasn't even trying to kill the brat. Imagine what I could do to him."

Stefan flinched. "You wouldn't."

"You know for a fact that I would, and you'll hear every bit of it."

"Fuck you."

"I'll have to decline that offer for now."

Stefan lashed out, trying to strike Axel in his evil, horrible, handsome face. Axel, well-trained in dodging blows, especially from Stefan, easily grabbed his hand, throwing him back onto the bed.

"Relax for now, darling," chirped Axel, confidently marching towards the door. "I'll be back in an hour to see if you've changed your mind. Oh..."

His silver eyes flashed with a sadistic fire. "And don't even think of transferring that Contract to anyone except me. If you do, I'll crucify your Russian friend and toss every brat in this camp onto a pyre."

Axel blew Stefan a kiss. "Tata, darling."

Stefan ran at him, but Axel was already out the door, and all he could do was fling his body against the wooden barrier, screaming in rage.

Chapter
TWELVE

1938

The years between the Breakup and the Black Foxes were a blur of anger, sorrow, and soul-searching.

Stefan might have compared it to his early days of homelessness, but while that Stefan Harkel had been searching for a home, the Stefan Harkel that marched out of Axel Lahner's apartment was just trying to escape. From Hitler, from the swastikas, from the ideology that had turned against him and his friends just as easily as his first family had turned against him.

Of course, it was impossible for him to find anti-Nazi spaces without being forced to interact with his old enemies. The communists, the Jews, the feminist women, the feminine queers he looked down upon.

Stefan Harkel was still Stefan Harkel: still violent, still a fascist, still a German nationalist who hated communism, but in the polite presence of people he had once despised, his disdain cooled. His fellow queers always greeted a quiet coming-out with a familiar genial relief that made him feel guilty for looking down on them. Women were not so terrible when he got to know them by helping them distribute flyers that called Hitler a monstrous liar.

Jews, in particular, he found that he had pigeonholed something awful because he never found two Jews that shared an ideology. Stefan still disliked Judaism, but he quickly discovered that Jews themselves were not a monolithic evil. They were just people.

And they were people that Hitler hated. Adolf Hitler, the traitor, the murderer. Even if Stefan had clung to his anti-Semitism in the years after the Night of Long Knives, he probably would have defended them still, because nothing made Hitler angrier than seeing Germans help Jews.

And so, whenever he could, Stefan stood up for them. If a shopkeeper refused to serve Jews, he would smash their windows and steal their goods. If Nazi thugs harassed them in the street, he would throw punches for them. As the years marched on and the Jews' rights were stripped away bit by bit, Stefan made sure he was always there, always stepping in, always fighting for them.

He was arrested often, and for a variety of crimes: distributing pamphlets that insulted Hitler, publicly insulting Heydrich, burning a swastika banner. But every time he was deported to Dachau, it was because he had defended Jews.

And every time he was sent there, it was Axel Lahner the SS officer that got him out.

Stefan would see Axel many times after The Breakup, both before and after Axel gave up on convincing Stefan to accept the SS as his new masters. Axel moved on, rising swiftly in the ranks thanks to his father's connections. He quickly gained all the power he needed to keep tabs on his ex-boyfriend, and he always knew when Stefan was in need of rescue.

Stefan would remember every one of Axel's rescues with perfect clarity, but none more than the last. When Axel saved him from Dachau for the third and final time.

The guards must have gotten sick of seeing Stefan Harkel, because they were particularly brutal that third time. When Axel came for him, he all but had to carry the prisoner bridal-style through the lying gates that boasted: "*Work Makes You Free.*"

Work didn't make Stefan free, but his ex-boyfriend's refusal to completely move on and abandon him did. And as usual, Axel took Stefan to his Munich apartment and barely said a word to him for a few days as he nursed him back to health.

And then, of course, after a few days of reprieve, he sat Stefan down in the living room and demanded that they *talk.*

"I don't think we have much to talk about," muttered Stefan, uncorking a bottle of stupidly expensive wine he'd pilfered from Axel's little kitchen and stretching out on the couch. Axel leaned against the front door, effectively blockading it.

"We certainly do," Axel muttered, fidgeting with a little copper medal on his chest, an award he'd been offered for four years of serving the SS. He was looking forward to graduating to a silver medal once he achieved twelve long years of service to the thousand-year-Reich. "And do you *really* think you should be drinking right now?"

"I'm thirsty," grumbled Stefan, feeling far too much like a teenage boy being nagged by his mother. He took a great big swig directly from the bottle just to offend Axel. It worked; the SS man winced.

"Then have some water," said Axel, almost pleading. Stefan slammed the bottle down on the side table.

"You're not the boss of me, *Untersturmführer*," he said, and Axel grunted like he did whenever Stefan insisted on calling him by his rank instead of his name.

"No," the *Untersturmführer* conceded before gesturing to the portrait of Hitler that scowled at the two men from above the mantelpiece.

"But the Führer *is* the boss of you whether you like it or not!" Axel cried. "You have to stop this, Stefan! You've already gotten a reputation as a Jew-lover, and I'm running out of favors to call in every time you get yourself tossed into Dachau! And this time, I was *barely* able to get to you in time! You need to cease this reckless behavior…"

"And become a good little Nazi like you," sneered Stefan, casting a scowl at Hitler's visage. Axel rolled his eyes.

"No, but you at least need to learn when to *be quiet.*"

"Ah, well," Stefan crooned, his voice dripping with bitterness. "Maybe you can teach me to *be quiet*. You're *great* at that, aren't you?"

"Stefan…"

"How's the bitch, by the way?"

Axel's brow wrinkled with annoyance. "My wife, you mean."

"That's what I said."

"Don't be like that." Axel's voice was at once pleading and genuinely aggravated, the sort of tone that a man who actually liked having sex with his wife might adopt if someone called her a bitch. It was Stefan's turn to roll his eyes.

"Just because you're playing games doesn't mean you have to defend her honor."

"She's a good person," Axel proclaimed. "She's very sweet. We're actually close friends."

"Marriage is picture perfect, then."

"It's a good marriage."

"A good *lavender* marriage. Bet it'd break her little heart if she learned you hate to fuck her."

"Maybe," sighed Axel with a shrug, glancing idly at Hitler's visage. He strolled over and turned the Führer's portrait around, as though to spare Hitler from having to witness such a crass conversation. "Nice thing about her, actually. She never asks for sex. Maybe she doesn't want it herself."

"Or you did such a bad job that she'd rather get it somewhere else."

That earned a snort from Axel. "Maybe. Either way, she's a good woman and a good mother. You don't have to insult her, especially when you don't even know her."

"Ah, good mother to the *spawn*. Right, forgot about them…" mumbled Stefan, prodding at the half-empty wine bottle and now completely avoiding Axel's gaze. He hated watching how his ex-boyfriend's silver eyes glazed over with paternal fondness whenever he spoke of his children. "How are they doing?"

"Very good," Axel said in the bright, tender tone that he had once reserved for Armin and Stefan alone. "Roza's walking. Helmut really loves cars, you know. Filled my damn house with these expensive little toys. I keep tripping over them. He's real sweet on Armin, too. Calls him his best friend in the world. They're really great kids."

"Good," Stefan said, his voice dripping with disdain. He was probably a horrible person for hating Axel's innocent little babies as much as he did. "I'm glad you're happy with your choices."

"Don't, come on, stop that," Axel said in a firm tone that was far too similar to the sort Wilhelm would employ when his soldiers drank too much. "I love my children, and I don't regret having them. If I have to choose between you and them, I *will* choose them. If I have to choose between myself and them, they'll win."

"I wouldn't ask you to leave your kids, shithead, but some honesty would be nice," spat Stefan. "Either tell them you'd rather have stayed with me, or tell *me* you're better off in your little lavender marriage."

"You're *such* an asshole sometimes, Stefan."

"I'm an asshole all the time, actually, I just don't hide it like you do. And you can pretend to respect the bi—" Stefan sighed in resignation and shoved his feelings aside. "*Brigette*, you can pretend to respect her, but you obviously don't since you won't even tell her that you don't love her."

"I *do* love her, just not the same way I love you," Axel huffed, sitting in the cozy chair across from the couch, sinking into the cushions and shaking his head. "And I *do* love you even though I frankly hate how you're acting."

"Jesus Christ, you *are* a father now."

"And a good one," Axel boasted with a smirk. "You'd really like Roza and Helmut if you met them, you know. Then you could stop hating them for existing."

"I fucking hate kids; you know that. Only kid I ever liked was my brother."

"All right, fair enough," Axel mumbled, his boasting smirk becoming teasing and too familiar. "I guess I'm biased because I didn't like them either until I had them. Plus, I get a nice little feeling of *schadenfreude* every time I see them. My brother and his *Schnuckiputz* haven't had any healthy kids, after all."

Stefan was just tipsy enough that he couldn't help but laugh. "Erich *still* calls her that? They've been married for one-hundred years, aren't they supposed to hate each other by now?"

"I hate them because they don't hate each other," Axel

chuckled. "Do you realize how lucky you are that you never had to meet them?"

"I'd rather go back to Dachau," said Stefan, utterly dry and deadpan, and Axel really laughed, laughed so hard that he clutched his stomach, leaned forwards, and that damn SS cap fell off his head.

"Don't say that, it's terrible!" Axel cried, and Stefan found himself smiling. He forced his vision to become even blurrier so he could steal this moment and pretend that Axel wasn't wearing an SS uniform.

"Next time you meet with Himmler, you should suggest that to him," Stefan suggested. "'*Reichsführer*, I have a brilliant new method for torturing Enemies of the State…'"

"*Stop…!*"

"Of course, if you show him Erich and Elfriede, then he'll want to kill himself…"

"Stefan!"

"…which suits me just fine, maybe that can be my next act of resistance: introducing your disgusting lovebird siblings to the hierarchy of the Reich."

"Stefan, stop it, I can't breathe!"

"That headline will be great. 'Führer Eats Twenty Cyanide Pills After Watching German Couple Call Each Other 'My Sweet Baby Mouse-Bear.'"

Axel laughed, and Stefan laughed, and they both laughed and laughed until their ribs ached and their lungs almost gave out. Stefan wished that they could have just sat there and laughed forever despite how much it hurt, because when they both stopped laughing, he had to see Axel in his SS uniform again. He had to see Axel give him a sad little smile.

"I really missed this, you know…" Axel muttered, and Stefan tried to feign casualness.

"We still fuck," he noted with a shrug, and Axel heaved a heavy sigh.

"I'd like it if we could do more than just fuck, Stefan, if we could…"

"You know what I'm going to say, Axel," Stefan decreed firmly. Hell if he was going to live in some plush apartment paid for by concentration camp laborers and blackmailed Jews. Stefan didn't know what the queer version of a mistress would be called, but he'd sooner castrate himself than live such a horrible, hidden existence.

"I'll leave her," Axel muttered, and there was a desperateness to his voice that made Stefan's heart ache. "If you really want that. I wouldn't want to publicly divorce, and I couldn't tell her the real reason, but I could…"

"Axel."

"I still love you…"

"Axel. *No.*"

"I know you still love me."

Stefan did, and he hated that he couldn't stop.

"Stefan…"

He did love Axel. But he hated the Third Reich more.

"You're fucking pathetic." The words left Stefan's lips, harsh and venomous. Axel stiffened. It wasn't the first time that Stefan had berated his ex-boyfriend, but he intended to make this dressing-down particularly brutal.

"Pathetic little queer simpering up to a Jew-lover even as you smash the Jews' windows and ship them off to concentration camps," Stefan declared, rising to his feet. "You're *pathetic*. Your father would fucking disown you if he found out what you were, yet you're so desperate for Papa's approval that you'll bend over for people who want you *dead* for the rest of your life."

"Stefan, stop it."

"Stop what?" sneered Stefan, traversing the sitting

area and leaning over Axel, who gave him a positively murderous glare. "Stop telling you the truth?"

"*Enough*, Stefan, I don't want to..."

"What *do* you want, *darling*?" Stefan crooned, harshly grabbing Axel by the chin and forcing him to look up. Silver eyes tarnished from years of serving Hitler glistened.

"I don't want to do this right now, Stefan..."

"Oh, I'm sorry, I forgot I was speaking to the great *Untersturmführer* Axel Lahner. You catch queers and ship them off to camps to be castrated and beaten to death and *raped*."

"Stefan, I'm serving..."

"The Reich, yes. Stopping degeneracy for the Reich." Stefan crawled into Axel's lap and felt his ex-boyfriend's body tremble.

"Stefan...stop."

Stefan would have never kept going in the past. *Stop* meant *stop*. But Axel deserved everything he got, and so instead, he leaned close as possible.

"But you *do* love being a degenerate, you filthy, hypocritical *faggot*."

Slap!

A hit in the face. Hard, as hard as the one that his father had given him on that last night in the Harkel household. Hard enough to send him reeling, hard enough to make him taste blood, hard enough to knock him to the floor. Stefan hadn't been expecting that because Axel Lahner was a Nazi, Axel Lahner was a monster, but Axel Lahner had never hit his lover even at his worst.

Stefan heard a rustling and a slight gasp and looked up to find that Axel, it seemed, was just as surprised as he was. For a moment the two men simply stared at one another, both gawking, both wide-eyed, both slack-jawed. Stefan quaked because he had been hit plenty of times in his life, but the last time he had been hit by someone he loved was when he was sixteen. Axel trembled and made a noise like a fish struggling to breathe on land.

"I...I'm sorry," Axel gasped. It would be the last time that Stefan heard those words fall from his ex-boyfriend's lips, and the last time he ever saw guilt flash in those silver eyes. "I...I didn't...I just..."

But Axel must have remembered himself, remembered who he was, remembered what he was supposed to be— merciless, unshakable, guiltless. He took in a deep breath and stood up straight, forcing his voice to become firm as he spoke with the cold forcefulness of an SS man. "Don't call me that again. Don't. *Ever.*"

Shock and trauma and all of those other weak unmanly feelings melted as a fire made of anger and lust erupted in Stefan's chest. He stood up and stepped forward, scowling right in Axel's face. The SS façade fractured as Axel blinked and tried to step back only for Stefan to grab him by his black tie.

"You're *not* in charge," Stefan declared. "I'll call you whatever I want, *Untersturmführer.*"

He dragged Axel into a kiss and pushed him back into the chair hard. The next few hours would be spent proving that he was in charge, always.

He still had sex with Axel because he wanted to. Because he wanted to prove that he was in charge, and because it was always nice to tear off that damned uniform and pretend like everything was still all right.

—————— ▽ ——————

Chapter THIRTEEN

1943

Hope was a rare guest in Stefan Harkel's soul, but he felt it once his anger abated. Alice had escaped, somehow, even though she must have been kept in much worse conditions. If she could escape, then so could he. It would certainly be easier for him. Not only did he know that Axel wouldn't allow his men to shoot him, but time was in their favor.

However Alice had escaped, her absence had surely been noticed right away. Axel had gone right after her without sparing time to discover *how* she'd gotten away, and then he'd found Stefan, whose presence would most certainly distract the Kommandant for a little while. The camp had a hole, and if Stefan and One-Twenty could slip through it before the Grandmaster plugged it, they could still win.

The little cell had a window. Barred with wrought iron, which meant that breaking out that way wouldn't be an option, but it offered a view of the camp.

The camp was small. The railway ran straight through it, cutting it in two, and there were a few barracks dotting either side. A cursory glance seemed to reveal that the prisoners were kept on one side of the tracks while the guards lived on the other, the SS barracks being decorated with lightning-rune flags and well-kept shrubbery.

Stefan and One-Twenty were almost certainly being kept in Axel's home since their building cast the widest shadow. That would make sense. The non-Masters were kept on the left side of the tracks until a train came to cart them off to Auschwitz or Treblinka, and any Masters that Axel happened to spot could be brought to his own personal prison and tortured until they surrendered their Contracts.

Stefan's eyes flitted to the right side of the camp, darting to the fence. Just one layer of barbed wire with watchtowers on each corner. No moat, minimal patrol. Made sense. There was no reason to have a lot of security on the guards' side of the camp, after all.

Just beyond the fence, it seemed that the camp had been constructed either on or next to some asshole's farm. There was a withered storage barn situated practically right against the barbed wire gate, and...

There, there it was! Hidden by the shadow cast by the barn, mere yards away from the building they were trapped in, there was a dip in the ground beneath the barbed wire fence. Alice must have crawled under. Stefan and One-Twenty would have a harder time than the emaciated girl if the fence were electrified. They would have to be exceptionally careful, but it would be possible to slip under the fence there, cut through the barn, and make it back to the woods. Home free.

Of course, that would require not only escaping, but escaping with the injured One-Twenty in tow.

Knock, knock, knock!

"Five?"

*Speaking of which…*Stefan ran to the thin wall that separated him from his comrade. "Hey, kid!" he cried, kneeling down and all but pressing his ear against the wall. "How's the Nazi hospitality treating you?"

"Terrible," One-Twenty replied in a dry manner that made it impossible for Stefan to tell if he was trying to joke or was just being blunt. "They did patch my leg up, though."

"How's it feeling?"

"I can still move it. Are you doing all right?"

"I'm fine, don't worry about me."

"They almost certainly took us alive to question us about the Black Foxes. I won't break…"

"I'm damn offended, kid. Are you suggesting *I* would?"

"No. I'm just concerned. If they find out how high-ranked you are…"

"It doesn't matter either way. The Kommandant doesn't want any information about the Black Foxes."

"He interrogated you already?"

"I guess you could say that…"

"What does he want, then?"

"Satan gave me a bunch of Nazi souls to torture forever because angels are too lazy and stupid to run Hell by themselves, and that little girl had Reinhard Heydrich's soul but gave it over to me, and now the Kommandant wants me to give it to him so he can give it to Himmler so they can all be murder buddies again."

A long, long silence, and then One-Twenty spoke: "How hard did they hit you?"

"Pretty hard," Stefan conceded with a chuckle. What he wouldn't give to be insane instead of involved in all of this.

"Are you still sane enough to think of a way out of this?" One-Twenty queried.

"Gotta idea already, but step one still needs to be sorted out. What's your cell look like?"

"Cot, no window, no bucket. Pretty typical. Had worse."

"When?"

"Ah, right, I guess I never did tell you about that. You know the rules about talking too much."

"We don't have much to do except talk right now, kid, and anything you could tell me about your miraculous escapes of the past could help us now."

"I somehow doubt it will be of any help," the Russian chuckled sadly. "It's kind of a long story, but have you ever wondered how me and Eight-Sixty became friends?"

"Not really. He's nice; seems like he could make anyone his friend."

"Ha! True enough, I guess. I got captured when I went after Naden, during that time when I disappeared for a while."

"I kinda figured. Eight-Sixty saved you?"

"His friend, actually. His friend was one of the SS guards. Franz."

"He had a change of heart?"

"Not really," sighed the Russian. "Franz was hiding Eight-Sixty at his farm and couldn't do it anymore because his troop was being relocated. He was desperate. Didn't want anything to happen to his one good Jew. He let me go on the condition that I save Eight-Sixty."

"And this Franz is still in the SS?"

"Far as I know."

"Hypocrite piece of shit," huffed Stefan. He hated Nazis in general, but none more than the Franzes of the world, the ones who shoved their own morals aside for the sake of love. Maybe it was noble to some people, but to

Stefan, it was the height of foolish, wicked hypocrisy. At least someone like Heydrich was *consistently* terrible.

How nice it would have been to be like Franz. How nice it would have been to squeeze his eyes shut and cover his ears and stay with Axel. To pretend like everything was fine.

"Don't say that to Eight-Sixty; he'll bite your head off," snickered One-Twenty.

"I have a really hard time imagining him biting anyone's head off."

"He can be tougher than he looks, especially when it comes to people he cares about. And he really cares about that Nazi…he really thinks Franz is a good person deep down. Thinks he's just confused and needs saving…"

"'I can fix him with love.'"

"Haha! Well, maybe not *quite* like that."

Clueless kid, thought Stefan with a sigh. He supposed all of that explained why Eight-Sixty had rejected his advances. Stefan hadn't thought that Eight-Sixty would have such a bad taste in men, but well, he really wasn't one to judge.

"Ah! Kommandant!"

Speaking of bad taste in men, thought Stefan, lifting his eyes to the ceiling as a series of extremely performative moans echoed from above. Apparently, the roof was thin enough to allow for noise leakage too.

"Shithead…" grumbled Stefan with a roll of his eyes, half tempted to jump on the bed, ram his fist on the roof, and shout at them to keep it down.

"Degenerates," grumbled One-Twenty.

"You have no idea," sighed Stefan, letting the expected homophobia roll off his back. One-Twenty wasn't entirely off-the-mark, even ignoring the queer issue. Axel must have known that Stefan would hear what happened up there, and he was sending a message. *I don't need you,* perhaps. Or maybe, *If and when we screw, your friend will hear everything.*

Stefan really hated the fact that he was already strategizing how he could screw Axel without One-Twenty figuring it out. The concept of having sex with a child-murderer probably should have been disgusting. He probably should have been catastrophizing about being touched by the same hands that would torture his friend or some poetic shit like that. But there were several good reasons to try even though Axel was going to at least *pretend* to not be interested.

It would be a distraction, for one. For him and for Axel. The Kommandant certainly wouldn't be willing to release them in exchange for sex. In fact, knowing Axel, he would be absolutely offended if Stefan even suggested such a thing. He would frown sadly and say something like, *You're not a whore, and I'm not going to take advantage of you like that.* Because for some moronic reason, Axel thought that torturing and killing Jews would affect Stefan less than if they just had sex and then called it even.

Still, it would at minimum distract the Kommandant for some time. It would give Stefan more time to plan. Maybe he could grab Axel's gun while he was undoing his belt or something.

Plus, Stefan hadn't had sex in well over a year, which for him was basically equivalent to torture. (No doubt when he died, his Master would punish him by forcing him to live multiple lifetimes of celibacy or something.) While he hated the thing that Axel had turned into, he did still love him. So that would be another good reason. Well, maybe not a good reason, but a neutral reason.

All right, that was a pretty bad reason. Fuck it. Stefan was probably going to Hell when he died anyway, and knowing what was waiting for him on the other side, he wanted to use his free will while he still could.

Hell! Axel had told him that he couldn't transfer the Contract, but he had said nothing about merely using it.

"I'm gonna zone out for a minute," Stefan said, and when the Russian promised to wake him if something happened, the God of Nazi-Land dove back into Zone N-1.

"Oh, oops," Stefan said when he emerged from the Master Room only to find that Heydrich was still on fire. Very much conscious, too, though his throat must have given out at some point since he was no longer screaming but merely gasping as the inferno refused to give him the release of death. Stefan almost regretted that he had the Zone set one-to-one with Earth's time. It would have been rather funny to leave Reinhard Heydrich in that state for what, to the Subject, would have been literal months of agony.

Stefan put the eternal fire out and barely gave the Hangman of Prague a second of reprieve.

"Heydrich," Stefan said, and he hesitated for a moment because he really *did* hate giving Commands, no matter how much they were deserved, but he didn't have time to spare. He inhaled sharply and summoned the most terrible power of the Contract.

"Tell me what you know about Axel Lahner." His voice echoed awfully, like he was speaking into a deep cavern. The Contract glowed scarlet.

The agony in Heydrich's eyes as his very soul was forced to act against his will probably should have been more appealing than it was. Monstrous as Heydrich was, as much as he deserved to be Commanded, there was still something deeply unsettling about the power of the Command. Stefan would much rather light his Subjects on fire, and he could tell that Heydrich would have preferred months of immolation over one moment of being Commanded.

"Husband of Brigette Lahner," Heydrich said, his voice halting and laced with pain. "Father of Roza and Helmut Lahner. Son of..."

"Yeah, yeah, whatever, I know all that!" snapped Stefan. "Tell me shit that's useful! If you needed to take him down, what would you do?"

"Likely utilize the fact that he's almost certainly a faggot."

Aha. "You knew about that?" Stefan said, not surprised at all. When Heydrich had been alive, it had often seemed like there wasn't a secret in the Reich that he didn't know about, that he wasn't squirreling away for later.

"Received several unconfirmed reports. Nothing as concrete as pictures."

"Why didn't you investigate further?"

"No reason to. Lahner was loyal. Also, didn't want a repeat of the Von Fritsch affair."

That earned a snort from Stefan. Axel had told him about *that* embarrassing little fuck-up. In an attempt to grab power from the regular army, Heydrich had searched for secrets and seemingly found out that the well-loved General Werner Von Fritsch was a homosexual.

As it turned out, however, the accusation had been leveled at a *different* Von Fritsch, an Achim Von Fritsch instead of Werner. When the details had been leaked of Heydrich's blunder, it had caused widespread humiliation for the Gestapo. It was only natural, then, that Heydrich would be hesitant to accuse any other comrade of homosexuality without rock-solid evidence.

"If Himmler found out what you know about Lahner, what would likely happen?" Stefan queried.

"Wouldn't know," replied Heydrich. "He can be testy. Might insist on Lahner undergoing some sort of therapy, likely at Dachau. I myself would have held onto the information until he gave me a reason to use it against him, but Himmler can be particular about these things."

"He wasn't *particular* about it when he pretended to be Ernst Röhm's friend for years."

"He wasn't pretending. I don't think he was, anyway."

"Not like you?"

"No."

"I don't know if that makes you worse than him or vice versa. Command's over, you can say whatever you want."

"Can I?" sneered Heydrich, sparing only a second to catch his breath after the grip on his soul loosened. "Can I call you a disgusting little faggot, then?"

"Wow. I can see how you got your dumb ass killed in Prague; you really have *no* self-preservation instincts. I gotta go. Don't hold up. Oh, uhm, and Reinhard Heydrich was lit on fire again."

This time, Stefan spared a moment to reset the Zone's time. One hundred years for every hour in the real world.

——————— ▽ ———————

STEFAN FIGURED OUT PRETTY QUICKLY WHY AXEL HADN'T put him and One-Twenty in the same room. He could hear One-Twenty scream, but he couldn't see what they were doing to him. That made it worse than it probably was. *Use your imagination,* Axel was practically saying, and Stefan did, and it made him want to die.

"Axel, you sick son of a bitch, stop it!" he demanded for the hundredth time. The hundredth time was evidently the charm, because at last One-Twenty's screaming stopped. Stefan might have feared that the Jewish lad was dead if he hadn't heard a smattering of Yiddish curses.

The heavy thud of jackboots informed Stefan that the SS men were leaving One-Twenty's cell and venturing upstairs into Axel's room. There was a moment of reprieve as Stefan asked One-Twenty if he was okay. ("No, but I've had worse," was the reasonable answer.) The two prisoners weren't able to speak for very long, however, as two SS men entered Stefan's cozy cell moments later.

"Hands in front of you."

"Fuck you."

Stefan did his very best, but the two guards easily overpowered him, pinning his arms to his sides and shackling his wrists in front of him with handcuffs. Stefan was dragged upstairs, spitting and cursing Hitler all the way.

They reached the second story, pausing in front of a sturdy door. The SS guards swiftly removed Stefan's shackles and shoved him into what appeared to be a small studio apartment. Axel was there, of course, sitting at a table set for two.

"Ah, fashionably late, I see. And so underdressed for the occasion!" the Kommandant chirped, his silver eyes sparkling. "It *is* our first date in a while. Sit, sit!"

Stefan grunted and gave his ex-boyfriend a scowl worthy of Heydrich, but nevertheless, he decided to obey.

Sitting across from Axel at the small dining room table made his gut writhe something fierce. They had screwed a few times since The Breakup, but they hadn't shared a meal since the good days. For a moment, Stefan thought that he would blink and be back in their apartment, joking about something Wilhelm had said earlier, chastising Armin for his relentless begging.

But he blinked, and he was still Black Fox Five, and Axel was still a monster.

Stefan glanced down, earning a chuckle from Axel when he grimaced upon realizing he'd been served soup. Spoon only, no knives, no forks, nothing he could steal and use as a weapon (well, maybe he *could* kill someone with a spoon, but probably not a well-trained SS man.) He slipped it into his pocket anyway, just in case.

He knew that Axel would notice if he let his gaze linger on any one potentially useful item, and so when he looked up, he blinked rapidly and inhaled sharply, distracting the Kommandant while he swiftly let his eyes flit about the room.

Vase. Mirror. Flowers. Plant. Desk. Typewriter. Pens. Letter opener.

Letter opener. Bingo, he just had to get Axel on that desk and make sure that the Kommandant would be too hot and bothered to notice if the Black Fox stole the letter opener.

Easy enough, Stefan thought, but perhaps he could use what Heydrich had told him to convince his ex-boyfriend to drop all of this.

"Eat something, please," Axel begged, folding his hands on the table and smiling cheerfully. "You must be famished."

"I'm a Master, you idiot," snapped Stefan, shoving the bowl away. "If you're going to try and convince me to come to your side with fancy food, it isn't gonna work. It's not like I can't get whatever I want in the Zone. Starving a Master's pretty damn hard. I'm still wondering how you managed to starve Alice."

"Oh, that was easy enough," chuckled Axel. "After all, she can't go into the Zone if her body is constantly being disturbed, and one of the first things they taught us in the SS was how to keep a prisoner from falling asleep even for a second. And if I was concerned that she might die of sleep-deprivation, we could just knock her out suddenly. Hardly an issue. Child's play."

"You should be happy you failed," Stefan said, grabbing the wine cup (not glass, so he couldn't break it and use the shards as makeshift daggers, damn Axel) and taking a casual sip. "If you'd succeeded and Himmler got his hands on Heydrich's Contract, you'd regret it."

"Oh? Enlighten me, darling."

"Heydrich knows you're queer, Axel," Stefan declared, leaning forward with a sneer. "If you give him to Himmler and Himmler Commands him to spill his guts, you're absolutely fucked. And if you don't hand him over to Himmler, then what? You keep him all to yourself and he's utterly useless."

Stefan rose to his feet, leaning over the table the way that the Gestapo interrogators always did whenever they captured him: palms planted flat on the *table*, eyes glistening with triumph. "You lose, *your majesty*, so give it up, let my comrade go, and we can have some fun and call it even."

"Stefan. *Please*," Axel replied, turning his chair slightly away from his ex-boyfriend, his silver eyes falling upon a map of the Reich that hung on a nearby wall. "Don't debase yourself."

"I'm not the one who debases himself in the bedroom, Kommandant," sneered Stefan, which earned him a derisive snort from Axel.

"I'm hardly desperate," retorted Axel, his eyes briefly flitting towards the open door to his bedroom.

"So I heard…" muttered Stefan. "Bet you get plenty of SS boys who are eager to please an important Nazi like you."

"Plenty," boasted Axel, grinning from ear to ear and folding his hands in his lap. Casually, Stefan started to circle around the table.

"Bet they let you do whatever you want," the Black Fox said. Axel maintained his braggadocious smile even though Stefan could see his confidence dribbling away.

"Anything," the Kommandant confirmed. He

squirmed but remained seated even as Stefan stopped right in front of him.

"Bet that's real boring," Stefan whispered, leaning close, too close, almost nose to nose with the Kommandant. Axel's cheeks flushed red, and his silver eyes shifted nervously.

"It is..." the Kommandant confessed. Stefan put a hand on his ex-boyfriend's cheek.

"*I'm* not boring," Stefan purred, and Axel let out a noise that was either a squeak or a snarl, shoving Stefan away and leaping to his feet.

"Stefan, stop it!" cried the flustered Kommandant, escaping from the little dining area and scurrying towards the corner of his pseudo-apartment that functioned as a living room. "I'm *not* going to do this."

"Why?" snapped Stefan, glancing at the desk and debating whether or not he could make it to the letter opener. He could have, but not without Axel noticing.

Stefan followed the Kommandant towards the little living area. "Don't tell me that little *actor* was enough for you..."

"I'm not going to take advantage of you like this," Axel snapped, plopping down on a cozy chair and crossing his legs. "It isn't right."

"Like you care about doing the right thing," scoffed Stefan, leaning against the wall by the fireplace and casting a scowl at the swastika-clad map of Germany.

"I actually *do*," argued Axel with a huff. "I put up with your rebellious silliness because I love you. And since I love you, I'm not going to screw you when you're not in a position to say no."

"You think you have all the power over me."

"I *do*."

"You've got way more on the little SS boy you screwed before."

"He's not you," Axel said, wrinkling his nose as though merely thinking about the other man made him disgusted. "I don't give a shit about him."

"I'd be shocked if you gave a shit about anything except yourself," grunted Stefan.

"Don't be like that. I could have ripped that little Russian's head off. I've been generous because I want to give you the opportunity to come to your senses."

"You still want Heydrich's Contract after what I just told you?" cried Stefan in disbelief, jabbing at the Hangman's Contract on his breast. Axel rolled his eyes.

"You'll have to forgive me for not believing you. It's more likely he just *suspected* that I was a homosexual. If he had solid evidence, Himmler would have already found it when he took all of Heydrich's files after the bastard kicked the bucket. An *accusation* could come from anyone, anytime, dead or alive."

Axel leaned back, proudly gesturing to the shimmering Nazi long-service award on his chest. "Once I give Himmler Zone N-1, I'll be far above mere *accusations*. After all, Heydrich himself was accused of being a Jew, and that wasn't enough to tear him down."

"He *wasn't* a Jew," Stefan noted. He, too, had heard the whispers about Heydrich's possible Jewish ancestry, but he also knew that had been little more than a rumor with no basis in reality. "You *are* queer."

"And so are you," Axel sneered. "And yet you still serve the Black Foxes."

"*You're* serving the SS!"

"I serve the winners, the right side of history," boasted Axel, gesturing towards his medals before waving his hand towards his injured ex-boyfriend. "*You* serve a scrappy group of rebels whose sole duty is to save Jews. A group of rebels who *explicitly* refuse to help queers."

That was true. The Black Foxes were primarily

devoted to saving Jews—mostly, as Papa Fox had rightfully noted, because the Nazis were mostly devoted to killing them. Made sense. No problem.

Still, the Black Foxes also tried to save other groups of so-called undesirables. Romani, disabled people, Poles, Slavs. On the radio, while Papa Fox mostly talked about saving Jews, he also urged his listeners to help those other persecuted people.

But queer men, they were left off the list. Papa Fox had never said a word in opposition to their treatment under the Reich. Stefan had asked Papa Fox about that once, why he never condemned the murder of queers, why he didn't beg his listeners to save the men branded with the pink triangle. Papa Fox had chuckled and said something to the effect of: *If Hitler only shoved criminals and freaks into those damn camps, we wouldn't have to exist at all.*

"I've always been willing to keep this side of me under wraps for the sake of a greater Cause, and for the sake of myself," Axel continued. "You, though...I don't understand you, Stefan. You gave up everything, everything I offered you, everything that made you happy...you gave *me* up..."

Axel inhaled sharply for a moment, paused to collect himself, and then let anger conquer his silver eyes once more. "For the Black Foxes. For the *Jews...*"

"For Jews, for queers, for women, for Jehovah's Witnesses, yes, for all of them, every person Hitler hates!" snapped Stefan, pushing himself off the wall and shouting so loud that the guards on the farthest border of Axel's camp could probably hear him. Axel's anger tapered into wide-eyed surprise as Stefan stalked towards him.

He stopped right in front of Axel, who was leaning all the way back in the chair as though he would have liked nothing more than to escape in to the cushion. Stefan planted his hands on each armrest and leaned so close to the Kommandant that they were practically nose-to-nose. "I'm not going to let Hitler have my soul again, and I'll happily give up anything to save the people he wants to kill, no matter who or what they are. *Anything.*"

Axel's response was quiet, morose and proud all at once. "That's my Stefan."

Stefan grabbed the Kommandant by his SS-rune decorated collar and snarled, "I'm not *your* Stefan."

Then he pulled him into a crushing, vicious kiss which Axel reciprocated with eager anxiousness.

"I told you I won't..." the Kommandant gasped when they broke apart and Stefan started undoing the buttons on his uniform,

"Shut up," Stefan snapped. "Treating me like I'm some helpless little boy who can't make my own damn choices. You need to remember who's really in charge."

"Y-yes..."

"Yes, *what?*"

"Yes, sir."

—— ▽ ——

STEFAN DID TRY AT LEAST A LITTLE TO DIRECT HIS EX-boyfriend towards the desk, but he couldn't be too obvious, or Axel would realize his mistake and put the letter opener out of reach. They ended up screwing on the couch, then in the bedroom, and once they were done, Stefan wrenched himself from Axel's arms and demanded to be returned to his cell.

"We still have more to talk about..."

"Either send me back to my cell or let me go."

"You're a manipulative bastard sometimes."

"Always."

"Cell it is. I'll leave the Jew alone for an hour, let you

think very hard about whether or not you feel like hearing him scream again."

That netted Axel a slap in the face, which resulted in a third round. After that and a brief shower (no damn razors in the bathroom either, maybe he could kill a guard with a toothbrush?) Stefan was sent back down to the prison. He managed to spit on the SS man who uncuffed him once he was in his cell, which earned him a harsh slap that sent him tumbling to the carpeted floor.

"Kommandant'll have your ass if you mess up my pretty face!" Stefan warned as the guard scurried out and locked the door behind him. Grunting, the Black Fox crawled to the wall and leaned against it.

Almost immediately, One-Twenty's voice greeted him. Never had he sounded more like a frightened kid. "I… Five…I was hearing…did *he*…did *you*…?"

Shit.

"Yeah, we did."

There was a horrible noise, a sob that was too much like the ones the Russian had let out during the week after his village was destroyed when he'd thought Stefan wasn't listening. "You…I'm sorry…I'm *so* sorry…"

That wasn't pity in his voice, it was *guilt*. Stefan felt like he'd been punched square in the gut because the poor boy was so sweet and so clueless. He thought that Stefan had agreed to screw the vile, disgusting, degenerate Kommandant in order to spare his young friend torture.

Stefan would rather have the kid hate him than know that One-Twenty hated himself.

"Don't, I did it willingly," Stefan said, and that one little truth was the crack that burst the floodgate. "I'm Stefan Harkel. I used to be in the SA before the SS killed my friends and I learned how stupid I was. That sick fucking Kommandant is my ex-boyfriend, and I screwed him even though he's a murdering bastard because I'm sick in the head. And I didn't want you to find out because I knew you'd hate me and…"

And on and on he went. The full truth, an account of his life from the moment he was kicked out of his home to the moment he joined the Black Foxes. He blurted it all practically in one breath because saying it all aloud made his chest tighten, and he knew that he needed to finish the story quickly or he would break and cry like a weakling.

"So there…" Stefan sniffled when he completed his tale by describing what he had felt when he'd found his first mass grave. "Now you know everything about me. And all that shit I said about the Contracts is true too, by the way. And I'm not crazy even though I wish I was."

"I…Five…"

"*Stefan*, please, for God's sake, I hate that number shit."

He expected *faggot, queer, degenerate*. He expected the soft voice to turn harsh as the lad started citing Leviticus and every other Judaic text that rendered Stefan Harkel a sinner.

He didn't expect One-Twenty to give a small chuckle and keep speaking in the same quiet, friendly tone. "All right, Stefan. If I'm going to call you that, though, you really should call me Sam."

"Sam…" Stefan uttered the name with disbelief. Among Black Foxes, the sharing of names was utterly forbidden. Only the closest of comrades, those who trusted one another as family, would ever divulge their name. Stefan had shared his out of frustration, but One-Twenty, *Sam*, had offered his as a sign of unbreakable friendship.

"Samuel Val," the Jewish man said. "I guess you already know my story. Most of it anyway. I guess I didn't tell you *why* I stopped hunting Viktor Naden."

It took Stefan some time to respond because he was

still so shocked by Sam's lack of vitriol. "Nah ah…I mean…I heard about his wife and daughter…"

"Black Fox Ten and Black Fox Twenty-Seven, yeah," Sam replied. Stefan himself had been away on a mission when Black Fox Ten, Viktor Naden's own wife, had been unmasked as a Black Fox operative and arrested along with her accomplice, Naden's eldest daughter. It hadn't been utterly shocking. Plenty of the Black Foxes' best agents were women and children, and it didn't matter how much Stefan bellyached about putting little kids in danger. Papa Fox would always say the same thing: *desperate times.*

"Before they were arrested, I ended up at their house with Eight-Sixty. After Franz freed me, I wanted to just plop Eight-Sixty off with the nearest Black Fox, and the nearest Black Fox happened to be Black Fox Ten."

"Pretty big coincidence."

"Not really. I'd gone to that area because I heard that Naden was spotted there. Guess I know why: that's where his family lived. Of course, at the time, I was pretty surprised. And…well…*angry* doesn't quite describe it."

"You obviously didn't kill them, though." Stefan knew he hadn't; Heydrich had. The report had gone out that Naden had somehow personally offended the Führer after his wife and daughter were arrested, no doubt by hypocritically pleading for his loved ones' lives. Hitler had ordered the Hangman to kill the two Black Foxes, and the Blond Beast had happily followed his command. A sad day for the resistance, and probably an even sadder day for the Beast of Belorussia, but completely unrelated to Samuel's quest for vengeance.

"Oh, I tried to do worse than kill him," Sam declared. "The Torah tells us that a man should be punished in the manner of his sin. *Ain takhat ain,* you've probably heard that phrase. An eye for an eye."

"I heard a lot more 'love thy enemy' as a kid, but I

always thought that was bullshit." Clearly, Stefan's mother wouldn't have had it in her to love her enemies if she couldn't even love her own son.

Sam offered a small hum. He was silent for a few moments before he spoke again. This time, his voice was the deathly hiss that Stefan had been anticipating. "Viktor Naden killed my entire family. Burned them to death."

Stefan was well aware that death wasn't the worst thing one could do to someone. Sometimes, it was comparatively merciful. "But you *didn't* kill Ten or Twenty-Seven..."

"I almost did," Sam confessed. "Waited until Naden got home, tied him up, tied his kids and wife up...didn't even care that Ten was one of us, that Twenty-Seven was one of us, I just wanted to hurt him. His youngest daughter was five."

"*Was...?*" Stefan knew nothing of the fate of Naden's youngest.

"She's all right," Sam assured him. "Eight-Sixty snapped me out of it. I dumped vodka on the kid, was holding a lighter above her head...I *almost* did it. If Eight-Sixty hadn't run out right at that moment and said the right thing, I *would* have."

Samuel's voice was hoarse, haunted, a tone that Stefan knew well: relieved guilt, the tone of someone who knew how far they might have gone if something hadn't flipped a switch in their head and made them say, *What the fuck am I doing?* It was a feeling Stefan was abundantly familiar with, a feeling that consumed him every time they found a dead kid and he had to look them in the eyes knowing that in another time, he might have been their murderer.

"So..." Sam sighed after a long stretch of silence. "I guess what I'm trying to say is...I was broken enough in the head that I almost killed a child. So after everything you went through, if still loving that madman is your biggest crime, I'm really not one to wag my finger at you."

Stefan wished that the wall was down so that he could give the damn kid the biggest, tightest hug in the world, a hug worthy of Wilhelm at his most paternal. But instead he let out a noise that was a choking laugh and pressed his side against the wall. "I guess we're all kind of fucked up, huh?" he asked.

"Me more than you," Sam replied, his typically serious voice verging on something resembling playfulness.

"Ha! You really think so?"

"You're a good person, Stefan," Sam said, his tone becoming resonate, the sort of tone worthy of a Rabbi. "If you weren't, you wouldn't be here."

"I'm an asshole," Stefan croaked. He really, really didn't want the kid to hear him cry. "You don't know what you're talking about."

"You're definitely an asshole, but you are still a good person even if you're a freak." Again, that almost-playful tone, the closest thing that a man as icy as Samuel Val could manage for a friend. Stefan laughed.

"Haha! Guilty as charged I guess."

"If you were a woman, by the way, I'd say the same thing. You have *terrible* tastes." It sounded like Sam was barely suppressing a laugh.

"The worst," Stefan concurred.

"Heydrich's wife has the worst."

Stefan laughed and made a mental note to tell his Subject as much the next time he saw him.

"Scratch that: *Goebbels'* wife has the worst," Sam said, and his tone, always so solemn, only made the quip even funnier. Stefan laughed, laughed harder than he had since the start of the war, laughed and laughed and let some of the tears that had been battering at his corneas escape.

"You are wrong, by the way," Samuel said once Stefan had stopped laughing. "And you're stupid."

"Tell me something I don't know."

"I meant about the hate thing, that I'd hate you for that," Samuel explained. "Not that I *like* it or *approve*, obviously, but you don't have to follow our laws."

Samuel paused for a moment as though to collect his thoughts, then let out a sigh so heavy that to Stefan it seemed to shake the thin wall separating them. "The laws of the Torah, you know, they're supposed to be a blessing, not a whip. It's a covenant, an agreement between the Children of Israel and *Hashem*. We're not supposed to force it onto the world. That's why we don't missionize. It would be stupid to hate someone for breaking a covenant they never agreed to. I don't hate my Christian comrades when they eat pork, and I don't hate you for what you do. It doesn't matter."

Maybe it was completely pathetic that a lack of utter contempt and hatred from this comrade made Stefan Harkel's heart break from happiness. Maybe. But fuck it. Nobody had ever told him that it *didn't matter*.

"I'm going to get you out of here," Stefan vowed before shoving his fist into his mouth so that Samuel wouldn't hear him sob.

———— ▽ ————

Chapter
FOURTEEN

1938

He snuck out of Axel's little apartment after they screwed. Escaping awkward post-coital conversations was a skill that Stefan had all but perfected. Axel had learned almost all of his strategies and had locked most of the potential exits, but he always forgot the bathroom window.

And so Stefan escaped through said bathroom window before his ex-boyfriend could wake up and insist on more damn *talking*.

He made his way back to his own apartment, which he owned more for convenience than a real need for a roof over his head. The Nazis had started shipping the perpetually homeless to camps in an effort to clean up the Reich's streets. Stefan preferred getting sent to Dachau for doing something violent or rebellious. Getting arrested for sleeping on a sidewalk? Boring. If Axel would inevitably get him out, he might as well go in for yelling that Hitler was an inbred piece of shit.

Of course, the price that Stefan paid for living in a shitty little apartment instead of a park bench outside a grocery store was ironically enough a lack of privacy. People knew where he lived, and so they knew where to find him. Axel, for one reason or another, was rarely a guest, maybe because he didn't want to be seen going in and out too often, or maybe because he insisted on "respecting" Stefan's space. Other SS men, of course, were less concerned about Stefan's comfort.

Thus, he wasn't entirely surprised when he woke up one day to a sharp knock on his door. A familiar sort of knock, the distinctive knock of a Gestapo man. The "open this door or else" knock.

Stefan preferred "or else." He knew that his landlord was a real ball of fire, and it was always funny to watch the chubby little man barrel down the staircase and scream, seemingly without an ounce of fear, right in the face of the strapping SS men after they grew sick of knocking and kicked down Stefan's door. *"One of you fuckers better pay for this!"*

And they always *did* pay for it, so Stefan considered letting the Gestapo kick down his door a little act of resistance in and of itself.

But this time, the person at the door knocked and knocked, and Stefan never heard a huff and a command to "break it down." Either the local SS troop had decided that they couldn't afford to keep paying for new hinges, or it wasn't the Gestapo.

Stefan, curious, opened the door and immediately recognized his guest.

"Herr—"

In a few swift movements, Stefan grabbed the man, yanked him into his apartment, shut the door behind him, and then slammed the guest against said door.

Friedrich Dressler opened his mouth, either to say

something or to shout in pain, but Stefan shut him up by clocking him across the face. The SD officer took the punch with grace, grunting, spitting blood, and dully muttering, "I deserved that."

"Give me *one* good reason not to beat you to death, you Nazi piece of shit! *One!*" growled Stefan, barely resisting the urge to just strangle Wilhelm's murderer before he could even get a chance to try and answer.

But Stefan took a good look at the SD officer, the weasel, and noticed that he didn't look the way that he had four years ago. Not that he looked *good*, there was a weariness in his eyes that remained, but his cheeks had filled out, his hair was actually well-kept, and there was something about his posture that made him seem completely different. No longer did he stand with the confidence of a member of the Master Race. Now, he held himself like all of the undesirable rebels that Stefan had encountered during his wanderings: with cautious determination.

"Well..." Dressler sighed, wiping the blood from his lip. "For one, I'm not a Nazi anymore. And from what I hear, that's something you and I have in common."

Friedrich's features became softer, more thoughtful, and he said in a voice that was too morose for an arrogant SS man. "Can we talk? Please? Then you can beat the shit outta me if that'll make you feel better."

The Stefan Harkel of four years ago would have laughed in Dressler's face before clocking him in said face, but that Stefan Harkel had been a Nazi. That Stefan Harkel had been an utter piece of shit who had helped Hitler rise to power and hadn't realized how awful Nazism was until it turned on him.

Stefan let Friedrich go, gesturing towards his hole-filled cozy chair. "Sit down and *talk*," he said, a command, not an offer.

Friedrich did, though he started not with an explanation but a statement. "You got out of Dachau again."

"Yeah," grunted Stefan, plopping down on a couch that he had found sitting near a dumpster which now sat opposite Dressler's chair. He'd either managed to get the smell out with five washings or, more likely, the scent of Dachau had rendered all other odors sweet by comparison.

"Heard you got thrown in for trying to help Jews," Friedrich mused.

He had. Stefan had gone to Vienna during the *Anschluss*, where Hitler finally "united" Germany with Austria. A bunch of Austrians who had clearly been chomping at the bit to finally consider themselves superior had yanked some Jewish women from their homes and forced them to scrub anti-Nazi graffiti off the streets.

Stefan had intervened, first of all because he had worked very hard on that anti-Nazi graffiti, and secondly because those Nazi assholes kept spitting on those crying women, many of whom were little more than teenagers. He'd taken a bucket of soapy water and tossed it right in those sneering Nazis' faces, and that had gotten him a brutal beating and a third trip to Dachau.

"Yeah, I did."

"Hm." Friedrich's eyes flitted about the barren little apartment before he queried, "How'd you get out?"

"I thought *you* were here to give an explanation," snapped Stefan.

"I am," Dressler vowed. "But I need to know. Please, you don't have to give any names. I just need to make sure that they didn't let you out because they got to you."

Stefan was rather offended at the accusation. He was half tempted to blurt out everything that had happened, to proclaim that he had given up more than enough to make sure that the Nazi infection wouldn't *get to him*, but instead he merely grunted a half truth. "Lahner got me out."

"I see…" Dressler said with a slow nod. "I suppose that makes sense. He still cares about you as a friend. It happens often, SS men standing up for their old friends who fall out of favor."

Friend. Friends. For a former SD man, he was pretty damn unobservant. Maybe he wasn't a Nazi anymore because Heydrich had fired him for incompetence. Either that or queers had some magical ability to sense one another that heterosexuals were blind to. That might explain why Axel was so good at hunting down queers he'd never even met.

Stefan didn't want to think of Axel, so he scowled hard at Dressler and spat, "Should I assume *you* fell out of favor?"

"Not exactly…" Dressler muttered, nervously raking a hand through his onyx hair. "I quit the SD. Quit the Nazi Party."

"What, conscience nagged you over what you did to Vogel and the others?" snapped Stefan, and Friedrich lifted his gaze, offering a cross expression.

"Look, I don't mean to offend you," he said in a genial but firm tone. "I know they were your friends. But I'm going to be frank: I don't regret killing them. I regret *why* I killed them."

"You—!" Stefan might have jumped to his feet and proceeded to punch Dressler's weaselly face another fifteen times, but the former SD officer raised both hands as though to surrender.

"I'm sorry," he said, and he actually *did* sound sorry. "But you have to realize that Vogel wasn't a good person. He was a Nazi. Did you read the shit he wrote?"

"The articles asking for queers to be accepted in the Party, you mean?" grumbled Stefan.

"Yeah, *only* queers. But he wanted women to be turned into breeding chattel, and he was calling for Jews to be stripped of everything and enslaved. I *know* you don't agree with that."

Stefan didn't. At the time, he had been so focused on the good things Wilhelm wanted—a strong Germany, widespread acceptance of queers—that he hadn't cared one bit about anything else. He hadn't thought about what sort of society he and Wilhelm were helping to build. He hadn't considered the fact that Wilhelm's utopia would have been Hell for millions of people.

He hadn't even thought about it, and as Dressler forced him to think about it, he tasted something sour on his tongue. "He didn't deserve to get shot for having shitty ideas..." Stefan muttered.

"No, not for having shitty ideas, but he did more than that. He was an SA Troop Leader. He didn't single-handedly build the Third Reich, but he was a brick in a rotten pyramid. I'm sorry that I killed your friend, but I'm *not* sorry that I killed a Nazi."

"You're a Nazi too," Stefan accused, and Dressler nodded before bowing his head.

"Yeah, I was. And so were you. And I guess we all got what we put into the world."

All. Stefan felt a brick form in his chest. "What happened to you?" he asked, and Dressler wrapped his arms around his stomach and squeezed as though even thinking about it all made him want to vomit. For almost a full minute, he didn't answer, and when he did, his voice was low and pained.

"They sterilized my sister," Friedrich said. "My little sister Ilse. She always looked up to me. I remember when she was little, she'd pretend to get kidnapped, and I'd play detective and rescue her just in time. Ha..."

Friedrich laughed hollowly. Stefan felt the brick in his

chest grow bigger and bigger. He had heard of the horrors of the Nazi eugenics program. Wilhelm had once declared that anyone with a disability should be put against a wall for the betterment of Germany. *In Sparta, they used to toss worthless little cripples off cliffs*, he had said. *We'd be wise to do the same thing.*

"Why did they sterilize her?" asked Stefan, his voice becoming gentle. Friedrich looked up, his almond-brown eyes flaring.

"She had epilepsy. *Epilepsy*, that's it. She wasn't…she wasn't broken until they broke her. They kicked down her door, dragged her to a hospital, knocked her out and sterilized her, and I…"

Friedrich paused for a moment, looking down at his own trembling hands. "I tried…before they did that…I tried to call in every favor I could. I tried to save her, but…it didn't matter. Heydrich threatened to demote me for even asking. Nobody was willing to let me have an exception."

Stefan hated himself for being such an asshole, but he couldn't help but say the worst thing he could right then: "Good."

Friedrich took it well, offering a smirk and a nod. "Yeah…" he conceded. "I remember after it was done, I was in the hospital bathroom. Looked at myself in the mirror, big SD man. I was crying because the doctors wouldn't do what I wanted. Crying like a little boy. And then I just looked at myself and thought, 'You piece of shit…how fucking dare you?' After everything I did for the Reich, all the people I hurt…and I never thought it was wrong until it affected me."

"I'm not sorry for you," muttered Stefan. "But I'm sorry for your sister. Is she doing all right?"

"She killed herself."

Shit. "Oh."

Not shocking. Violated in such an awful way, mutilated against her will. And in the new, glorious Germany where a woman was only worth the number of perfect Aryan babies she could pump out, Ilse Dressler must have truly felt that her life was over. No place in the Reich, no place in the world.

"It's my fault," Friedrich declared with a hiccup, and while that was true, the better part of Stefan's soul forced him to refrain from kicking the ex-SD officer while he was down.

"You did *try* to save her, even if that makes you a hypocrite…"

"And I failed," said Friedrich, his quivering voice becoming firm and furious. "And I failed because of this rotten Reich that I helped build."

For a moment, there was silence as Friedrich's words made the brick in Stefan's chest unbearably hefty.

At last, Stefan asked, "Why are you here?"

"After Ilse…after she…I almost did the same thing," Friedrich confessed, turning his face away as though the shame was unbearable. Then, however, a small, soft smile tugged at his lip. "But, ah, there was already someone on the rooftop I picked. A Jewish woman."

"Ah." Stefan knew that smile decorating Friedrich's face. He'd seen it in a mirror once. Seeing it on a face that he hated made him yearn for Dachau.

"Dr. Ben-Ami," Friedrich said, dropping the title with such pride that it might as well have been his own. "Apparently, a lot of Jews kept going up there and tossing themselves off, and since she couldn't practice medicine— woman and a Jew, you know—she decided that the best way to save lives would be to sit up there and talk to anyone who came up."

"Sounds like a nice lady."

"She's amazing." Friedrich's eyes were really twinkling now.

"Talked you down?" Stefan assumed, and the former SD officer nodded.

"Yeah. She was pretty curious why a Nazi was up there. We talked a lot, before and after I officially left the SD. And we, ah…well, we're very close."

"Holy shit," grunted Stefan. "Just say you're screwing her, don't be such a prude."

Stefan almost crackled up as Friedrich's infatuated smile morphed into an expression of horrified humiliation. "I-I-I am not!" Dressler squeaked, but then he seemed to think carefully and gave a small nod. "Well, I am now, but…agh! Anyway!"

Friedrich threw up his hands. His face was roughly the shade of a tomato. "We're married now, but it turns out her father's a Rabbi. We went to France so I could get his approval, so he could marry us. Very nice fellow, and tremendously understanding. I was talking to him, and I mentioned that it felt wrong to just walk away from it all with a shrug after everything I did to build the Reich. I mentioned that I wished I could do something to really make up for everything I did."

"And…?" Stefan prodded. The crimson hue dissipated from Friedrich's face as his expression became serious once more.

"He introduced me to someone. A close friend of his who has the means to really change things, to really help people, to get under Hitler's skin."

"Help people?"

"Look…" sighed Friedrich. "I don't expect you to like me or to trust me. But things are bad now, and they're only going to get worse for Jews, for people like Ilse. Austrian Jews can't get out, and now Hitler's taking the Sudetenland. You think he'll stop with that? No. He'll take the rest of Czechoslovakia, and then he'll go for Poland. And I'd bet fifty Marks that the Allies will roll over like a dog and let him have everything he wants. And even if they don't, there will be war, and it'll be even harder to get people out. And Poland has *millions* of Jews."

"And this 'friend' of yours has a brilliant idea to save them."

"Little by little. Using his connections, we can smuggle as many as we can to safety. But we need all sorts of people to make it work. People like me, I'm good at finding people. People like you, you have guts and heart, and I know you wanna crack some skulls. You've survived Dachau three times. You're strong. We could use you."

"Who is this 'we'?"

And one year after that, Stefan Harkel was Black Fox Five, standing near a pit of murdered children, his heart burning with righteous fire.

———— ▽ ————

Chapter
FIFTEEN

1943

"All right, Reini, am I gonna have to use a Command, or are you gonna be nice and compliant?"

Stefan gave his Subject a moment to catch his breath, to recover from the ordeal of being immolated for a few centuries. Heydrich must have been used to such punishments from his last three Masters because he only needed a few minutes to get used to not being in indescribable pain before he inhaled sharply and turned to the God of Nazi-Land with a scowl.

Stefan, who was once again sitting on Heydrich's sprawling desk, tapped the Contract twice as a warning. Heydrich must have decided that being recalcitrant wouldn't be worth the pain because his icy eyes filled with resignation and he muttered, "What do you want to know?"

Stefan, being an asshole himself who was currently the

God of the biggest asshole in the Third Reich, decided to push. "What do I want to know...?" He waved his hand in a circle like a teacher faced with an unruly student. Ever-proud Heydrich bristled, but he glanced at the Contract, winced, and gave in.

"What do you want to know, *Master?*" the Hangman snapped, and Stefan hummed cheekily.

"Hmmm...you know, first, I'd like to see some groveling."

That was apparently too much for Heydrich. "Go to Hell, faggot," he snapped, and Stefan replied with a chuckle.

"Hate to point out the obvious, but..." The God of Nazi-Land gestured about the false office in Heydrich's little corner of Hell and then tapped the Contract again, another warning.

For a man as haughty as Reinhard Heydrich, bowing before an undesirable was probably nearly as agonizing as being burned, but he did it anyway. Stiff and trembling with rage, he prostrated himself before the God of Nazi-Land, pressing his prominent forehead against the ornate carpet.

"Good dog," chirped Stefan. "Now, I know you kept a lot of files in hidden places. Do you have any hidden files that might have been incriminating for Axel Lahner?"

"No." Stefan almost wanted to Command Heydrich to get up just so he could see his face, which must have been positively red with anger and humiliation.

"You seriously had nothing on him?" scoffed Stefan.

"If he's queer, he covered his tracks well. As I said, it was all rumor, nothing stronger than the Von Fritsch case. No pictures, no truly reliable witnesses."

"Shit. All right, you can sit up."

Heydrich did so, remaining on his knees. The

Hangman hesitated for a moment, squirming as though something was writhing about in his gut. The Head of the Gestapo was a naturally curious man, however, and so he couldn't help but ask, "Why do you want to know so much about Lahner?"

Stefan grunted and almost refrained from answering, but he decided that Heydrich wouldn't be able to do any harm with the information. "He's holding me captive, and he wants your Contract."

"That's possible…he could take the Contract?" Heydrich muttered, his tone taking on a lilt of eagerness.

"Only if I give it to him," Stefan sneered, leaping off the desk and slowly marching back towards the Master Room. "Don't get your hopes up; that isn't happening. No matter what, I'm not letting him get your Contract. I'm just trying to see if I can convince him to drop this whole scheme for his own self-preservation."

"And if you can't?" Heydrich asked, his hopeful tone becoming biting. Stefan stopped just in front of the Master Room, turning around to fully face his Subject.

"If I can't, then I'm gonna have to find some other way to make sure he doesn't get the Contract," Stefan declared, tapping the sun-colored triangle on his breast. Heydrich rose to his feet, dusted himself off, and gave Stefan a poisonous smirk.

"Well…" sneered the Hangman. "You could always kill yourself, faggot."

Stefan once again could only respond with a sigh. "This is a waste of time…"

"I have all the time in the world," Heydrich muttered bitterly, and Stefan smiled, his eyes glowing gold as he summoned his powers.

"All the time to burn," the God of Nazi-Land declared. Hopefully, he would eventually get to the point where his head was clear enough that he could be more creative with Heydrich's punishments.

—————— ▽ ——————

"SAM, CAN YOU WALK?"

Stefan heard a brief skittering of footsteps on the other side of the wall. "Yeah."

"Can you run?"

"I think so."

"Be ready to. Follow my lead, all right?"

"You got it."

With Sam's cooperation assured, Stefan abandoned the wall and hopped onto his bed, ramming his fist on the roof and screaming, "Axel, you piece of shit, I wanna make a deal! Bring me up now!"

Axel must have been listening closely because in practically the blink of an eye, Stefan was being shoved into the Kommandant's quarters.

"You've finally come to your senses, then?" Axel said, putting out the cigarette he'd been smoking and offering his ex-boyfriend a smile that was at once fond and vicious.

The Kommandant was sitting at his desk, and the letter opener was still there. *Perfect.*

Axel opened his mouth, no doubt to gloat or something to that effect. Before he could even hope to say a word, however, Stefan grabbed him by his tie and dragged him into a deep kiss that obviously startled the Kommandant as much as it thrilled him.

It only took a few swift movements. He shoved Axel onto the desk, keeping a grip on him with one hand. In another quick motion, he knocked the pen holder off the desk, but not before grabbing the letter opener and tucking it into his sleeve.

Stefan was keenly aware that he could have slit the Kommandant's throat right then. If someone had asked him why he didn't and he'd cared about their opinion, he would have spouted some bullshit. *That would just put the camp on high alert. He's got good reflexes. It wouldn't be worth the risk.*

But the truth of the matter was that Stefan still loved Axel Lahner. So instead, he commanded his ex-boyfriend to take the damned uniform off, ignored his protestations about "stalling" and "taking advantage," made sure to carefully take off his jacket so that the precious letter opener wouldn't fall to the polished floor, and indulged for some time. He let himself pretend that they were still in their apartment, that he would hear the patter of Armin's paws at any moment, that he was back in that short, horrible, happy time.

———— ▽ ————

"All right, we really need to talk now. Enough stalling."

"You seemed to enjoy that stalling quite a bit."

"That's beside the point," Axel huffed, straightening out his rumpled uniform like the proper little prince that he was before turning to Stefan. The Black Fox had put his clothes back on, making sure that the letter opener was still secure.

"You said you wanted to make a deal," Axel said, crossing his arms behind his back. "So out with it. What exactly do you have to offer me?"

"Myself," Stefan said, placing a hand over the Contract and sitting down on the edge of the bed. "Forget this whole Heydrich scheme. Let my friend leave this place, and in exchange, we call it a draw. You don't get Heydrich's Contract, but neither do the Black Foxes, and you don't risk Heydrich airing out everything he knows about you. Lord knows how many hidden files he has tucked around the Reich that Himmler *didn't* find after he croaked. Is it really worth the risk?"

"Are you being serious?" Axel said, sounding absolutely aghast at the idea. "You're offering to be my prisoner? You think I want to chain you to the wall? You think I *want* that?"

"Well, it might be fun," mused Stefan, smirking as Axel let out a frustrated snarl and threw his hands into the air.

"Unbelievable!" cried Axel. "You really have a low opinion of me, don't you?"

"Says the child-murderer," retorted Stefan venomously, and his ex-boyfriend's silver eyes flared like fire from purgatory.

"Jewish whelps are *not children!*" snapped Axel, slamming his hand against the wall and gesturing towards the covered window. "No more than a newborn rat is a child! I have tried one thousand times to explain this to you, Stefan, but you're so hard-headed and emotional that you just don't *get it!* I swear, it's like you *are* a woman!"

"Was that supposed to be an insult?" chuckled Stefan, shaking his head. "Have you met the women of the Black Foxes?"

"Ha!" Axel growled, looking away from his captive ex-boyfriend and fidgeting with his SS long service award. "Oh, yes, I'm sure the Black Foxes attract plenty of dykes!"

"Considering what you were doing a few minutes ago, Axel…"

Axel let out a sound that was at once a growl and a scream. "God, you're infuriating!"

"And you're inconsistent," Stefan noted, jabbing his thumb towards the blinds, towards the camp they hid from view. "You loyally serve an ideology that wants to find a 'cure' for homosexuality. You send other men, fellow queers, to camps where they get castrated and tortured and raped until they get 'cured.' Do you really believe in all that Nazi bullshit, or are you just a self-serving traitor?"

"I *do* believe in it!"

"All of it? You think queers should be 'fixed'? You'd be happier if you weren't queer?"

"*Yes!*" Axel's answer was practically a shriek, all pain and desperation. Stefan had known Axel's feelings for years, but hearing the obvious announced aloud still hurt.

"That's fucking pathetic," Stefan hissed.

"Maybe…" Axel said, hastily rubbing at his eyes, inhaling sharply to regain his composure. "But it's what I believe. It's what *you* used to believe."

"Bullshit," retorted Stefan. "I don't wanna be 'fixed,' and even if I didn't like Jews before, I never thought they were literal demons. I believed in the SA once, but I was an idiot for doing so. Even if Wilhelm got what he wanted and the movement accepted us, it would have been wrong because he still wanted to hurt Jews."

"Oh, God forbid!" Axel snarled, shooting a murderous glare at the blinds. "God forbid the sweet, precious little Jew pigs get *everything* they deserve!"

"You know, I wish I could see inside your head and figure out how you deal with all the hypocrisy floating around in there. You think Jews are evil…"

"They *are*, Stefan! Wilhelm knew that!"

"Wilhelm was wrong."

"You can't turn against the Reich because of him and then at the same time say he was wrong!"

"I sure as Hell can. He was wrong about the Jews. So was I. Almost every idiot in Europe's been wrong about them for most of history. Or do you really believe that

Jews poison wells and eat matzo made of Christian blood?"

"I don't believe in *medieval* anti-Semitism, but the fact that Jews are responsible for manipulating markets, corrupting culture, and spreading degeneracy is a *proven fact!*"

"'Spreading degeneracy,'" snorted Stefan. "What, so you think the Jews turned you queer?"

Axel grimaced, glanced at the window, and muttered something about science and history. Stefan cackled.

"You're so fucking stupid, oh my God!" he cried. "And such a hypocrite! You think Jews are evil and cause degeneracy, you think queers should all be *cured*, and yet you're still head-over-heels for Stefan Harkel the queer little Jew-lover."

"I'm not a hypocrite!" Axel snapped. "I've said it over and over: I wish you were a woman, and I wish we were both normal. And if that's impossible, then I'll do what I can in my capacity for the Reich, for Germany, and if I have some fun on the side, it more than evens out. I've had children, I've fought the plague of Jewry, and I don't very much feel like slapping a pink triangle on myself and letting the doctors try to fix me when I'm not actively spreading degeneracy."

"I'm sure Himmler will be very understanding when Heydrich spills his guts about your *fun on the side.*"

"I *still* don't believe what you're saying about Heydrich's knowledge, and I don't believe you made this deal in earnest. You're still stalling, trying to save your little Jew friend!"

"You're breaking my damn heart, your majesty. Being rejected by such a *prince*. My self-esteem is shattered. I thought you wanted to get back together with me. Divorce your wife and keep me nice and hidden in an apartment for some *fun on the side*. Isn't that what you wanted?"

"It's not!"

"So what *do* you want?"

"I can't get what I want, all right?" Axel yelped, slapping a hand over his own Contract. "The only place I get what I want is the Zone, and that's not fucking real!"

"Oooh," chuckled Stefan, idly brushing a thumb over the Hangman's Contract. "Now I'm curious. What *do* you do in the Zone when you play out your little fantasies? Did you make a little Prop of me, have a little puppet that looks like me swear my eternal love for you and Hitler, run to you and beg for forgiveness…"

"*No,*" Axel insisted, his shoulders sagging, sadness consuming his eyes. "I don't want some empty husk. I'd rather have nothing than something that isn't real. And I won't force you to pretend that you want me again."

"Who's pretending?" asked Stefan, jabbing his thumb towards the open door. "I think every piece of furniture in this apartment can testify that I'm not pretending to want you. I'd have to be a damn good actor."

Axel flushed red and gave Stefan an incredulous look, shaking his head. "You're saying you want to get back together?"

"Yeah. I do." Stefan couldn't have hoped to fake the genuine sincerity that leaked into his voice. "You're a piece of shit, but I still love you, and I know you still love me even if you don't want to."

"Stefan…" Axel covered his mouth with his hands, released a shuddering breath, and glanced at a swastika flag that hung on a nearby wall. "It's not about what either of us want. We're on different paths. I love you, but it doesn't matter. I'm going to do what's right, and you're going to do what you think is right no matter what you want."

Stefan knew that, but hearing it aloud still hurt. Slowly, he nodded. "Yeah."

"This is a waste of time," Axel observed, brushing a hand through his perfect dark hair and plopping his SS cap on his skull. "You're going back to your cell, and you're not coming out until I'm the God of Zone N-1. If I have to skin that Jew boy alive, I'll do it."

"I know you will," Stefan muttered. With a shout, Axel summoned an SS officer into the room, who quickly hand-cuffed Black Fox Five. Axel watched him restrain Stefan's hands with a grimace.

"Please stop making this difficult," Axel said, half a command, half a plea.

"I make everything difficult," Stefan retorted, numbly letting the SS man lead him from Axel's little room.

He barely heard Axel's soft reply. "Yes...you do."

———— ▽ ————

PATIENCE WAS NOT A VIRTUE THAT STEFAN HARKEL WAS accustomed to, and so it was dreadfully difficult for him to let the SS man drag him down the staircase and back into his cell. It was difficult for him to wait until the SS man had shut the door behind him, pulled out the keys, and removed his handcuffs.

Then, and only then, did Stefan strike. The letter opener was in his hand and then, just as quick, lodged in the SS cadet's throat. The guard gargled and choked, and Stefan yanked the letter opener from the Nazi's neck and put him out of his misery with a swift strike through the eye. If he deserved to be tortured for all eternity, well, his name would appear on someone's Contract, maybe even Stefan's. Absent that, Stefan was only willing to torture Nazis that he knew deserved it.

Quickly, he got to work stealing the SS man's clothes. Stefan was almost tempted to dress the Nazi in his own scrappy outfit and put him under the blankets. He refrained, however. The massive pool of blood on the floor would alert any SS man that came to check on him that he had escaped. He settled for donning the grey uniform and stealing the gun.

Idly, as he slipped out of his cell and tried every key to open Sam's door, Stefan realized that he had broken his vow. *I'd rather fucking die than put on that uniform.* Desperate times, like Papa Fox always said.

He finally managed to open the cell door, revealing a threadbare room with a blood-soaked prisoner.

Sam's bullet wound had been dressed, thankfully: Axel had no doubt wanted to keep his hostage alive lest he lose his best play against the God of Nazi-Land. The Jewish man jumped to his feet, which was good; he would be able to run. Defending himself, however, would be a hurdle even if they could find him a weapon. Sam's right hand was bandaged up, and his left hand was missing three fingernails. Stefan hated the fact that he knew they would grow back in about six months, give or take.

"Let's go," Stefan said, taking his stolen gun from its holster. "Stay behind me, I've got you."

Samuel nodded and obeyed, following Stefan slowly, grasping his ribs all the way out the door. Quite fortunately, the Russian was silent as a rabbit, and even more fortunately, no dogs barked. Maybe it was feeding time, or maybe they were just too accustomed to only chasing Jews on the other side of the camp. Maybe Axel had even gone through the trouble of making sure that the hounds learned to ignore Stefan's scent lest his handsome face get mauled when he inevitably tried to escape.

And that, of course, would be their biggest problem: Axel knew Stefan too well. He almost certainly knew that his ex-boyfriend would try to escape. The barn might have even been a trap, but it was still their best chance. They had to get there, then break for the woods once the sun set and darkness gave them cover. It was already dusk. They could make it.

The Black Foxes kept to the shadows, hugging the Kommandant's building as they slunk towards the dip in the fence. Stefan finally found a use for the spoon he'd stolen earlier by chucking it at the fence, confirming that it wasn't electrified. Cheap Nazis evidently didn't want to supply that much power to a small camp in the middle of nowhere. Their loss. Or rather, Axel's loss. *Hopefully* it would be Axel's loss.

They crawled under, Sam with some difficulty; the Jew hissed in pain when the barbed wire scratched at his back and snagged his jacket. Nevertheless, they made it under and swiftly ducked inside the barn, discovering that it was not filled with Nazi officers just waiting to capture escapees. No Nazis, just sacks and sacks of grain stamped with swastikas and reminders that the produce was strictly for the Reich.

"Piss..." Stefan mumbled when he tried the door on the other side of the barn and found it locked, perhaps by the farmer or maybe an SS man. He looked up and spotted a second story to the barn. Even without seeing a window, he could tell there was one up there. He could see weak sunlight spilling into the barn from above.

"Up, quick," Stefan commanded, and Sam obeyed without question, following Black Fox Five up the rickety, slim staircase to the second story.

Said second story was filled with a few empty boxes, some bags of expired grain that were covered in dust, tools, sheets, and a few odds and ends piled near a small window.

Stefan threw open the window and looked down. A clear shot to the woods, and the sun was nearly down. Jumping down, of course, would probably be a bad idea if they didn't want to break their legs. He could only imagine how insufferably smug Axel would be if he found the two Black Foxes lying helplessly in the mud with shattered femurs.

"Hey, Fi—err, Stefan, you think we can survive that fall?" Sam asked. Stefan stepped back and shrugged.

"Survive, sure, but we'd have to drag ourselves back to the Bunker, and I'm not sure if I can elbow-crawl faster than a German shepherd."

"Remember when we were going through Poland, and we jumped from the second story of that burning building and landed in the dumpster?"

"Don't remind me. Cushioning my fall with dirty diapers is *not* a fond memory."

"No trash here to use as cushioning, but..." The Russian grabbed a sack of grain, tore it open, and tossed the contents out the window. "Second best thing?"

"Not a bad idea, kid," Stefan chuckled. "Let's get to work. We have to be quick: Axel's gonna notice we're gone soon."

And so they hastened, dumping all of the grain sacks that were on the second story. When they ran out of expired bags, they started carrying sacks up the stairs and dumping those.

Samuel really had an admirably stubborn spirit; he carried the heavy bags even though it was clearly agonizing for him to do so with his injuries. Stefan had always known he was that way, though. He remembered the days after he'd first found Samuel, when the Russian had, even when nursing a near-fatal bullet wound above his heart, kept pace with the rest of them, fought harder than any of the other Black Foxes, and never once complained.

Then again, willpower was often the best pain-suppressant.

After a few trips from both Stefan and Samuel, they

managed to amass a decent-sized pile of grain that would likely pad the fall of at least one man.

"Maybe one or two more," Stefan said, breaking open a bag and leaning out the window, "Then we'll..."

Stefan all but swallowed his own tongue when he looked outside and saw a pair of headlights breaking through the darkness as a car pulled right next to their little pile of grain.

Axel emerged from the vehicle alone. Perhaps he had chosen to come by himself out of arrogance, or perhaps it was out of concern that one of his more trigger-happy underlings might kill Stefan. The Kommandant looked down at the grain pile and then looked up, his snide smile wide enough that Stefan could count his teeth even from a distance.

"Shit!" he cried, leaping back.

"What's wrong?!" Sam yelped, coming up the stairs with another sack of grain. Stefan grabbed his comrade by the shoulders and yanked him behind one empty crate.

"Axel Lahner, the Kommandant," he hissed. "He's coming inside."

"The gun?" Sam suggested right away. Stefan yanked the Luger from its holster and cursed when he checked it. The Nazi he'd killed must have just shot a prisoner or two since the gun only had two bullets left, and since Stefan was a horrible shot, he would probably miss twice.

"Fi—Stefan, what's the plan?" Sam queried, and if he was afraid, his tone didn't betray it at all. It seemed like he really believed that Stefan would know how to get them out of this.

Stefan would much rather die than disappoint his young friend, but his brain whirled and whirred and sputtered. They could jump and run, but no doubt Axel would then call for reinforcement and they would never get away.

They almost certainly wouldn't be able to take Axel in a fight, especially since Stefan doubted he could ever hurt Axel.

A high-pitched goat's voice echoed in his ears, and the Contract thrummed. *You could always kill yourself.*

Stefan gritted his teeth. The prospect was more than tempting despite the fact that he still disliked the notion of active suicide, but he didn't know if that would work. Did a Contract disappear as soon as the Master died, or would it linger, ready for Axel to snatch it up and present it to Himmler?

But then...then Stefan realized that he had two Contracts. And an idea struck, desperate and stupid and entirely too dependent on Axel's affection overwhelming his desire for Zone N-1. And maybe if he'd thought about it more, if he'd had more time, Stefan could have come up with something better, but right then he realized that he had two Contracts. And as long as he kept one, Axel would be none-the-wiser for a little bit.

"Here," Stefan said, shoving the gun into Sam's arms. "Keep that. Don't use it unless you absolutely have to. I need you to promise to do exactly what I tell you, all right? No matter how insane it is. Swear on your holy book."

Sam didn't hesitate, putting a hand over his heart. "On the Torah, I promise, what do you want—? Stefan!"

Two swift motions from Black Fox Five made the Russian cry out in shock. He tore the Contract to Zone N-1 from his breast and whipped out the letter opener. Sam, of course, could not see the Contract, but he certainly saw Stefan slice at his own hand.

"Stefan, what the Hell?" Samuel hissed, immediately starting to rip off a part of his shirt to dress the wound. *Sweet kid.*

Stefan's emergency pencil had been confiscated when

he'd been captured. He could only hope that the Contract wouldn't be picky.

"I renounce the Contract to Zone N-1."

Apparently, it wasn't picky, because there was a flash of golden light as he used his own blood to cross out his name.

"I renounce the Contract to Zone N-1…"

"Stefan, what are you…?"

"I renounce the Contract to Zone N-1!"

The golden light that consumed the Contract and erased Stefan's blood-splattered name obscured Sam's shocked expression for a second. When the Contract suddenly appeared before the Russian's eyes, he threw himself back against the crate and yelped, *"Hashem…Hashem…!"*

"God, exactly, yes!" snapped Stefan, who had learned the Hebrew term for God long ago, when he'd heard it uttered by desperate, dying men in Dachau. Stefan smeared some of his blood onto the slack-jawed Jew's bandaged hand. "Now sign it, quickly! Remember your vow!"

Sam winced and obeyed as though God Himself had used the power of Command upon him, only managing a two-letter initial on the dotted line. It was good enough: the blood turned black, and Sam shuddered as the power of a God became his.

"Okay, now here!" Sam cried, attempting to toss the Contract back at Stefan. Of course, this only resulted in the Contract folding itself back into a triangle and flying at the Russian, sticking to his breast and eliciting a yelp of shock from the young man.

"Gevalt!"

"Hush, listen to me!" Stefan commanded, and Sam slapped a hand over his own mouth and nodded.

"This is my most important order. I need you to keep

that Contract away from the Nazis, away from Axel Lahner. Nothing else matters. Do you understand?"

"N-no, but I'll listen. I won't let them get...whatever this is," vowed Sam, placing a hand above his Contract-clad heart. Stefan saw the steely determination in the Russian's bright blue eyes and felt a bolt of hope strike his heart. Somehow, he knew that Samuel would keep his word.

"Good." Stefan sighed. "Then stay here and be ready to run, kid."

"What about you, though?" asked Sam, looking at his commanding officer with big, worried eyes that were far too much like those of Gerhard Harkel.

"Stefan!" Axel's voice rang out as he entered the barn. Stefan took a deep breath and smiled, patting the Russian's shoulder.

"Don't worry about me, kid. I'm gonna distract him. You go when I give the signal. Run for the Bunker and don't look back."

"Signal...what...?"

"*Stefan!*" Harsher this time. "Are you going to make me call for backup, or can we resolve this civilly?"

Civilly. Stefan almost laughed, but instead he stood. "You'll know it when you hear it," he whispered to his friend. "Good luck, Sam."

For once in this life, he was grateful for the religiousness of his comrade, for Samuel could not disobey Stefan without breaking a vow made to the Lord. The Russian stayed where he was, clutching the Contract to Zone N-1, while Stefan descended the staircase.

"Ah! There you are, sans one Jew." Axel, decked out in his full SS uniform—frightening ash-grey coat, blood-red swastika, shimmering long-service pin, the works—flashed a handsome, devilish smile at his ex-boyfriend as the former God of Nazi-Land blocked off the staircase with his body. Briefly, silver eyes flitted to Stefan's breast, and the Kommandant nodded once when he saw a Contract still glittering over Stefan's heart.

"Did you already send your Jew running?" chuckled Axel. He pulled something out of his pocket, a small silver whistle. "Bad idea. I'd never sic the dogs on you, but on *him...*"

"And lose your little hostage?" Stefan said, earning another vicious laugh from the Kommandant.

"Oh, I realize your little Jew must be a particular sore point for you, Stefan, but I'm patient," Axel chirped. "We get plenty of Jew whelps, and while I'd rather not make you watch anything too *nasty*, you're really beginning to force my hand."

"You would have just been disappointed if I gave up," Stefan said, a small smirk twisting at his lip. "That'd be boring."

"And you're certainly not boring," noted Axel, fondness entering his voice before his arrogant smile wilted and his gaze flitted down to the bloody letter-opener in Stefan's hand.

"You really had to go and kill poor Peter, eh?" sighed Axel sadly. "His parents will be inconsolable..."

"Don't pretend like you give a shit about him."

"Needless killing doesn't appeal to me, Stefan."

"*Ha!*"

"I won't pretend to be to be broken up, but I notice that you killed that poor, stupid teenager instead of slitting *my* throat." Axel smirked that insufferably, princely smirk of his. "I'm flattered, and you really should be ashamed."

"I'm pretty shameless, you know that," Stefan said with a roll of his shoulders.

"Utterly. Now, since it's clear that you're stalling..."

"Axel, stop!" Stefan barked before the Nazi could

touch the whistle to his lips. Axel did, lowering the whistle and grinning at the Black Fox.

"Give up, finally?" he said, dropping the whistle into his pocket and pulling out a pencil. "All you have to do is hand it over and I'll let your little friend go."

Stefan would have thought that this moment, a moment he had expected to come suddenly and brutally, would, if drawn out like this, be torturous. But strangely enough, Stefan felt light, liberated in a way that he never had. When he lifted up the letter-opener and gave Axel one final way out, he found that he didn't care at all that he knew he would be rebuffed.

"One last chance, Axel," he declared. "My offer from before still stands. Take it, or you'll regret it."

Axel laughed. Stefan wished his laugh would have become as terrible as the rest of him, but no. Same laugh. "You're kidding me, Stefan. You're barely even bringing a knife to a gunfight, and even if you were..."

Axel's expression softened. "I know you'd never hurt me."

"No," Stefan confessed. "Too bad that feeling isn't mutual, huh?"

"Stefan..."

"That's a no, then? Final answer."

"That's a no, Stefan," Axel confirmed, his voice bright, his smile confident.

Stefan laughed, and Axel's smile faltered.

"Stefan?"

"See you in Hell, Axel."

And in one swift motion, Stefan buried the letter opener into his own heart.

"STEFAN!"

Stefan wouldn't feel very much after that. It hurt, sure, but the pain was intense enough that the world became black quickly. When he heard Axel scream his name, he knew without even hearing Samuel obediently leap out the window that he had won. Axel was too panicked to even think of Heydrich, or Zone N-1, or anything except the dying love of his life.

It was nice, actually, to die in Axel's arms, hearing his frantic sobs. It was one final assurance that for all the hate that Stefan Harkel had put up with and put into the world, he at least died loved.

▽

Chapter SIXTEEN

"The prisoner is dead, Herr Kommandant."

The camp doctor delivered that decree with the nonchalance of a man discovering that the badger he'd struck with his car was indeed dead. Kommandant Lahner's entire world stopped. He dug his nails into the bottom of the cheap wooden chair he'd been sitting in just outside the infirmary and shook his head.

"That isn't true..." Axel whispered, and the doctor shrugged.

"I'm afraid we couldn't resuscitate it."

It! Axel leapt to his feet and grabbed the doctor by the lapel, shaking him brutally. "He is *not* dead! You didn't try hard enough! You didn't try!"

"Sir, I did!" yelped the doctor, utterly terrified by this sudden change in his typically affable superior's demeanor. "I know he was important, sir! I promise I tried!"

Reality struck Axel like a ton of bricks, and fiery anger became a frosty numbness. He slowly released the doctor.

"Yes, he was..." whispered the Kommandant. "He

was important. I'm sorry...please...go to your other duties. I need to..."

Axel stumbled into the infirmary without bothering to come up with an excuse and barely heard the SS doctor's frightened footsteps as he eagerly fled the scene.

A part of Axel had always worried that he would one day be called to a morgue and find Stefan under a sheet, but at the same time, his Stefan always seemed to dodge death by millimeters. Perhaps he wasn't the most fortunate man on planet Earth, but Stefan Harkel had undoubtedly had a guardian angel watching over him given how often he'd escaped his own Judgement Day.

But Death had finally come to collect, and Axel slowly trudged towards the covered corpse, peeling the sheet away from his ex-boyfriend's face.

Stefan had once joked that if he died, he wanted to be an ugly cadaver. *Women, they wanna be pretty corpses,* he'd laughed after a particularly brutal brawl with some communists. *Not me. I wanna go out with bruises and scars. Closed-casket funeral.*

Axel wasn't sure how he was going to have a funeral for his love. He certainly wouldn't be burning him in the open pit with all the worthless Jews that died before they could be shipped off to Auschwitz or Treblinka. Perhaps he could have a little coffin built, although a closed-casket funeral wouldn't have been necessary in any case: Stefan was, in fact, anything but an ugly corpse. Aside from a slight bruise on his cheek and the unearthly placidness of his face, he looked as handsome as ever.

Ultimately, Axel would force some Jewish slaves to fashion a casket of spare wood. He would bury Stefan just outside the camp, under the shade of a tree. Then he would return to his duties, his heart freshly unburdened, awash with a sense of liberation that perfectly matched his sorrow.

But right then, Kommandant Axel Lahner grasped Stefan's open-casket-worthy face with both hands and pressed his forehead against his.

"Why did you do that, Stefan?" the Grandmaster sobbed. "It wasn't that important…it wasn't that important…"

▽

Samuel Val made it back to the safety of Black Fox One's hideout by the skin of his teeth. He ran and ran, refusing to stop, eat, sleep, or check his wounds, haunted by an ever-present sensation that the Nazis were nearly upon him.

When he finally did reach the Bunker, Sam collapsed inside and was passed out for three days. When he finally awoke, he told his comrades what had happened, leaving out, of course, the Contract.

There was a brief period of mourning for Stefan among Sam's comrades, but the Black Foxes could not afford to dwell on their dead while the living still needed help. And so they reorganized Stefan's troops and left Samuel to recover with his best friend at his side.

"Hey, is your leg okay?" queried Black Fox 860, known to Samuel by his real name, Amos Auman. The Black Foxes' chief babysitter fidgeted with the end of his turquoise scarf, his equally turquoise eyes glinting nervously.

"Feels better today," sighed Sam, his eyes flitting from his friend to the sun-colored triangle stuck to his chest.

"Five…" Amos started to say.

"Stefan."

Amos seemed confused for a moment before understanding overcame his turquoise irises and he smiled gently. "Stefan would be glad to know that you're all right. I could always sense that he liked you a lot."

"He was the one who saved me when Naden…" Sam took in a shuddering breath, and Amos placed a comforting hand on his friend's shoulder.

"It's been a while since we lost someone that was really close to me," Samuel muttered. "I never get used to it."

"Never," Amos concurred. "But please don't feel guilty about it. He always knew what he was getting into and was always willing to take a risk for strangers, much less someone he cared about. He was a good man."

"I know that. I just hope he knew it," muttered Sam, tracing the Contract with his nailless fingers.

"Is your heart feeling alright? You've been kind of… looking down and touching that area for a while. Is your wound acting up?" Amos asked with utmost concern. For a moment, Sam did feel that old bullet wound burn, something that hadn't happened since he had stopped hunting Viktor Naden. He looked at his friend and lifted up a curious brow.

"You…don't see this?" Sam said, gesturing to the strange, magical paper above his breast.

"See what?" Amos queried, peering closely at his friend's chest and then shaking his head when he evidently failed to see the Contract. Sam, who had been too stunned and numb to examine the golden paper, lifted a brow and chewed on his tongue.

"Hey…Amos, do you mind if I have some privacy for a minute? I think I need to rest," he begged, and his friend immediately complied, wishing him sweet dreams and leaving him alone in the chilly Bunker room.

Once Amos was gone, Sam plucked the strangely warm paper from his chest and unfurled it. He read the gothic font quickly.

**THE LORD HAS GIVEN THEE
A POWER KNOWN TO ONLY HE
THE POWER OF COMPLETE CONTROL
OVER THIS, A HUMAN SOUL
UNTIL THE MOMENT OF REPENTANCE
AND THE END OF THEIR SENTENCE
THE ONE WHO SIGNS THIS
CONTRACT
IS HEREBY THE MASTER OF
ZONE N-1
AND THE FOLLOWING SOULS CONFINED THEREIN:**
Reinhard Tristan Eugen Heydrich

Samuel read it over three more times. If he hadn't been holding the Contract, feeling the way that it beat like a living heart in his hands, he might not have believed it. If he hadn't seen the unearthly glow that had flashed when Stefan had summoned the golden paper out of thin air, he would have dismissed this as a childish prank.

But Stefan had spoken quite soberly about a Contract offered by Satan that gave him ownership of the Blond Beast's soul, and Sam suddenly realized that every word of his friend's ramble had been true.

Samuel Val held the soul of Reinhard Heydrich in his hand. The Man with the Iron Heart. The man in charge of the *Einsatzgruppen.* The man ultimately responsible for every death that Samuel had been forced to endure, from his family in Khruvina to Stefan, who had died to keep the Hangman's soul from falling into the wrong hands.

Anger filled Samuel's heart. Burning, blistering anger. The sort he hadn't known since that day in Naden's house. All he could think right then was that he wanted to be in this Zone, acting as a God, making Reinhard Heydrich *pay.*

Sam barely felt himself fall, so consumed was he by his

own thoughts. He felt a brief sensation like he was diving from a tall building, and then he was sitting on a silver throne in a strange room, with his fingernails back where they belonged and his wounds seemingly healed.

Curiosity won out over anger for a little while as Samuel explored the room, lingering before the misty mirror, somberly gazing up at Stefan's portrait, and studiously reading the Manual until his eyes ached. The Jewish man came away well-informed as to what he had become and what he needed to do.

The God of Nazi-Land walked down the hallway and confidently strutted out the door.

"Ah. Another new one."

It was not the first time that Samuel Val found himself face-to-face with Reinhard Heydrich. Once, he and Amos had joined Black Fox One on a mission to infiltrate and destroy a concentration camp that the Hangman had built for captured Black Foxes. Samuel had agreed to be part of that dangerous mission out of duty, yes, but also because he had desperately wanted an opportunity to spit in the face of the man who had destroyed his life.

And now, as he stepped into a sprawling office and found himself staring down the sneering Butcher of Prague, it was Samuel Val, the sole survivor of Khruvina, that had all the power. And Heydrich knew it even though he rose from his desk and offered his new God a scowl.

"So, what are you supposed to be?" the Hangman asked, but then his icy eyes twinkled with recognition. Samuel had heard that the Butcher of Prague had a photographic memory, and it seemed that rumor was true.

"I've seen you before," Heydrich observed. "You were with Black Fox One."

Samuel gestured for Heydrich to step away from his desk. The Hangman gritted his teeth and curled his black-gloved hands into tight fists but nonetheless obeyed. They stood a few feet away from one another, the Nazi and his victim.

Samuel crossed his arms and confidently proclaimed, "I'm your Master now."

Heydrich's eyes flared frostily for a moment, as though he would have liked nothing more than to deny that statement, but then his stiff shoulders slackened slightly in resignation. "Yes, you are," he said, and it sounded as though that admission hurt as much as any torture.

Sam's bright blue eyes flitted to the floor. "Kneel down."

Heydrich did not, crossing his own arms, bristling like an irate cat. Maybe he was merely trying to cling to what little freedom he had left, or maybe he hoped that Sam was too green to know about Commands.

But Sam had read the Manual, and he knew what to do. He solidified his will and projected it onto his Subject. The Contract glowed red, and Sam's voice boomed like that of the Lord at Sinai: "***Kneel down.***"

Heydrich did, trembling and gasping as though the pain was so intense that he couldn't even let out a scream. Once, Sam had been forced to kneel at the Hangman's feet. Now, the tables had turned.

"***Don't move,***" Samuel Commanded, and Heydrich didn't, barely breathing.

Slowly, the Jewish man strutted up to the Nazi. An indescribable but familiar feeling filled Samuel's heart, and it was a feeling that might have frightened him if he'd been able to focus on anything except Heydrich right then. Heydrich in pain. Heydrich degraded. Heydrich getting everything he deserved.

Samuel spat directly on the Hangman's face. He could feel Heydrich's humiliation and pain as he wasn't even able to lift up a hand to wipe the Jew's spittle off his cheek.

"You can talk," Sam said with a sneer, relishing this

divine power. "You know, you slaughtered my entire family."

"Good," Heydrich hissed, his tone at once furious and agonized, as though he was barely resisting the urge to cry. "I hope they suffered."

"They did," declared the God of Nazi-Land, rolling up his sleeves. "And you're going to suffer ten times as much. *Ain takhat ain.*"

Epilogue

"One minute in Purgatory? Really? I figured the sodomy would get me at least a year."

The late Stefan Harkel sat on a small chair in the midst of a grand courtroom, or at least it was supposed to be a courtroom. In actuality, it was a vast dark space occupied by two desks, a projector, and piles of film reels. A moment ago, the Court had been presided over by the very Eye of God which had watched as two angels argued about what should happen to the eternal soul of Stefan Harkel.

Ha-Satan had made the case against Stefan while an Archangel in a white cloak had acted as Stefan's defense. Stefan had sat in the courtroom for what felt like literal decades but was surely only a second in reality, maybe even less. Time was malleable in the afterlife, after all.

Stefan felt no hunger or exhaustion, and his joints never became stiff as he sat and watched the Archangels play reel after reel of films that showed his entire life from the moment he turned thirteen to the second of his death.

The Archangels would fast forward through the long

stretches of nothing, and then pause when Stefan did something, anything, that could be construed as either a merit or a sin. The two divine lawyers (there was an oxymoron, he mused at some point, *divine* lawyers) would cite divine statutes and commandments in their pursuit of convincing God to either let Stefan into Heaven or damn him to Hell.

And Stefan had been braced for Hell. There had been a lot of sin in those film reels, after all. A lot of screwing married men. A lot of violence and alcoholism and cursing God's name. A lot of activities that his mother had warned him would result in eternal damnation.

And yet it hadn't, because there had also been a lot of rescued children, a lot of dying men given comfort, a lot of helpless people defended. The Defense had declared that it would be a crime to let a man as good as Stefan Harkel spend more than one minute in Purgatory.

And the Judge, whom Stefan had cursed many a time, had actually *agreed.*

Ha-Satan, it seemed, was rather happy to have lost his case. "Most souls have to spend some time in the Furnace," the Archangel said, shutting his briefcase and looking up at Stefan. His mirror-mask offered the deceased man a view of his very soul, which didn't look much different from the body he had known: messy dark brown hair, ragged clothes, and brown eyes that glistened with surprise at the result of his trial.

"Almost all of them, actually," the Prosecuting Angel mused, reaching down and touching the upside-down triangle on his chest. "You're getting almost nothing because at the end of the day, you were a good man."

Stefan had never felt like a good man, not once in his entire life. Having morals and adhering to them, in his mind, was not *good*, it was *neutral.* At most, his actions had been an attempt at balancing the scales, making up for the fact that he too had once been a cog in the creation of the Third Reich.

But Ha-Satan had no reason to flatter him. Stefan was pretty sure he didn't have a heart anymore, being an incorporeal soul and all, but he still felt it do a little back-flip. "You're gonna make me blush…" he muttered with a forcefully careless laugh. "You're just saying that because I worked for ya."

That fetched a chuckle from the Prosecuting Angel, who dusted off his desk. "I'm not so biased, though I'll admit that it *is* a shame we lost you so soon. We try to keep Masters in work for as long as possible. You were a good one, too. Ah, well. Let's get you to the Furnace quickly. In and out, and then you can enjoy Heaven."

With a snap of his gloved fingers, Ha-Satan summoned a silver door. Stefan hopped off the small chair and prepared for whatever brief punishment he would receive on the other side of the door, but before he could even get near it, Ha-Satan held out an arm to stop him.

"Hm…although…knowing you, you might find Heaven boring after a while," Ha-Satan mused. Stefan had never thought that he would be in a position to judge Heaven at all, but now that he considered it, an eternity of peace and tranquility *did* sound like his very definition of tortuous boredom. He nodded.

"You enjoyed your work as a Master, yes?" Ha-Satan queried, which definitely seemed like a lawyer question. Stefan, however, assumed that he was protected by some form of Heavenly double jeopardy, and so he chose to be honest.

"Yeah. Any way I could continue it?"

"Unfortunately, no," sighed Ha-Satan. "We tried that initially, making dead souls Masters. The results were… bothersome. However, there *is* a way that you could serve Heaven and have some adventure in your afterlife."

"Serving Heaven? Don't care. Adventure? Let's hear it."

Stefan's distorted reflection in Ha-Satan's mask briefly smirked as the Prosecuting Angel snapped his fingers and banished the silver door.

"Every once in a while, a soul escapes from where it's meant to be," Ha-Satan explained. "A Subject who escapes their Master, a sinner which escapes Judgement, a Husk that evades extermination. Us angels sometimes have trouble finding these as it's difficult for us to think like humans do. Therefore, we have an elite troop of humans trained to track these rogue souls down even in the very depths of Hell. The Rogue Hunters."

Ha-Satan strolled back towards his desk and leaned against it, and briefly, Stefan could have sworn that he saw Heydrich's office in the Angel's mirror mask. "What do you say, Herr Harkel?" Ha-Satan asked. "Think you could make it in the Rogue Hunters?"

Stefan didn't hesitate. "Sign me up, Chief."

———————— ▽ ————————

To be continued in *Aliza in Nazi-Land*.

Historical Notes

Although *The Hangman's Master* is a work of historical fantasy, many events and facts portrayed in this book are based on real history.

Concerning the SA Purge and the role of homosexuals in the SA:

Homosexuality had been illegal in Germany long before the rise of the Nazis, in particular male homosexuality. In the aftermath of the First World War, however, gay life in Germany, especially in Berlin, achieved something of a hidden renaissance. While homosexuality was still officially illegal, the law forbidding homosexual relationships was rarely enforced. "Police…found that it was hard to enforce Paragraph 175 since illegal sexual acts were committed privately."[1]

Nonetheless, homosexual men still faced hatred and persecution, and most chose to keep their lifestyles hidden

---

1. Bhatt, Goral, "The trajectory of male homosexuality in Nazism" (2021). Master's Theses and Doctoral Dissertations. 1096. https://commons.emich.edu/theses/1096

from friends and family. Some, however, were less secretive. Amongst them, longtime friend and comrade of Adolf Hitler, Ernst Röhm. "Ernst Röhm, the SA leader, developed a political ideal based on hypermasculinity and masculinist homosexuality. He valued traditional values of masculinity, like honor, honesty, obedience, courage, and 'comradeship.'"[2]

Hitler was, indeed, aware of Röhm's homosexual lifestyle. He did 'tolerate' it, either out of friendship or selfishness. "Hitler was fully aware of most if not all of the loose morality in the Nazi leadership...He did not openly encourage it, but did little or nothing to stop it. Hitler was part panderer, part avuncular father confessor. In his more mellow, less lonely moments, he regarded his 'Old Fighters' who were his personal retainers as part of his family."[3]

When complaints reached Hitler about homosexual activities within the SA, he would state, "Some people expect SA commanders...to take decisions on these matters, which belong purely to the private domain. I reject this presumption categorically...[The SA] is not an institute for the moral education of genteel young ladies, but a formation of seasoned fighters. The sole purpose of any inquiry must be to ascertain whether or not the SA officer...is performing his official duties...His private life cannot be an object of scrutiny unless it conflicts with basic principles of National Socialist ideology."[4] Many other members of the Nazi Party also knew of and tolerated Röhm's activities (In a letter to Rudolf Hess, Martin Bormann wrote: "I have nothing against Röhm as a

____

2. *Id.*

3. LEPAGE, JEAN-DENIS. *Hitler's Stormtroopers: The SA, the Nazis' Brownshirts, 1922 - 1945.* FRONTLINE BOOKS, 2022.

4. Heger, Heinz, et al. *The Men with the Pink Triangle: The True, Life-and-Death Story of Homosexuals in the Nazi Death Camps.* Haymarket Books.

person. As far as I'm concerned, a man can fancy elephants in Indochina and kangaroos in Australia—I couldn't care less."[5])

While the number of homosexual men in the SA is often overstated as a result of propaganda spread by Hitler's rivals, it is beyond dispute that Röhm's nepotism led to him installing many homosexual men in positions of power within the SA. "Rohm…gathered around him his old clique composed of a dissolute crew of adventurers, men with a reputation for corruption, debauched perversion and violent criminality. Sadists, drinkers, old friends and opportunistic young male prostitutes…bound to him by strong ties of loyalty."[6]

This drip-down led to some disaffected young homosexuals joining the Nazi Party under the banner of the SA, ignoring or excusing the contradictions between Nazism and acceptance of homosexuality by hoping that Nazism would eventually evolve to "embrace the concept of a Männerbund society, presented by a psychologist Hans Blüher in his book *The Role of the Erotic in Male Society*. Blüher argued that same-sex affections between males provided superior social and political cohesion, more than that of a heterosexual family."[7] Thus, because of Ernst Röhm, "Though Nazism repulsed many gay citizens, Röhm attracted some homosexual Germans to early Nazism."[8]

However, this would not last. As stated in this book, a conspiracy would form to oust Röhm from power shortly

---

5. *Id.*
6. LEPAGE, JEAN-DENIS. *Hitler's Stormtroopers: The SA, the Nazis' Brownshirts, 1922 - 1945.* FRONTLINE BOOKS, 2022.
7. Bhatt, Goral, "The trajectory of male homosexuality in Nazism" (2021). Master's Theses and Doctoral Dissertations. 1096. https://commons.emich.edu/theses/1096
8. *Id.*

after Hitler became the German Chancellor. "The beginning of the fateful year 1934 saw a difficult impasse develop between Röhm and Hitler…Röhm's attitude now became openly hostile. Recklessly, or with unbelievable naivety, Röhm made barely-veiled threats, and attacked Hitler's conservative allies, including the Army, and senior Nazi Party functionaries in frequent speeches."[9]

Seizing upon this tension, Röhm's rivals within the Gestapo and the SS, namely Heinrich Himmler, Hermann Goering, and Reinhard Heydrich, would "use every opportunity and means to drive a wedge between Hitler and Röhm, even going so far as to accuse Röhm, as Hitler's only serious potential rival, of planning a coup against the Führer. At long last, Hitler was forced to conclude that the SA, unruly and undisciplined, headed by a man whose objectives threatened his own, simply had to go. Operation Kolibri (German for "hummingbird") was on."[10]

Operation Hummingbird, now known as the Night of Long Knives, would see the SA leadership arrested, including Röhm, who, after refusing to commit suicide, was shot in his prison cell. Estimates of the number of deaths from the Purge fluctuate between one hundred to several hundreds, but the brutality is not in question. "All over Germany the liquidations began on the night of 29/30 June and continued throughout the Saturday and Sunday. SA senior officers and leaders were arrested, some summarily executed by SS death squads."[11]

In the aftermath of the Purge, in addition to claiming that Röhm's supposed treason provoked the slaughter,

9. LEPAGE, JEAN-DENIS. *Hitler's Stormtroopers: The SA, the Nazis' Brownshirts, 1922 - 1945*. FRONTLINE BOOKS, 2022.
10. Plant, R. (1987). *The Pink Triangle*. Mainstream Publishing.
11. LEPAGE, JEAN-DENIS. *Hitler's Stormtroopers: The SA, the Nazis' Brownshirts, 1922 - 1945*. FRONTLINE BOOKS, 2022.

Hitler would make a heel-turn and use Röhm's homosexuality to sweep his murder under the rug. "I should like every mother to be able to allow her son to join the SA, [Nazi] Party, and Hitler Youth without fear that he may become morally corrupted in their ranks. I therefore require all [surviving] SA commanders to take the utmost pains to ensure that offenses under Paragraph 175 are met by immediate expulsion of the culprit from the SA and the Party. I want to see men as SA commanders, not ludicrous monkeys."[12]

Concerning the pink triangle and the treatment of homosexuals after the purge of the SA: with the SA leadership in tatters after the 1934 Purge, the SS, Hitler's fanatical personal guards, took their place as the de facto army of the Nazi Party. This granted new power to the viciously homophobic leader of the SS, Heinrich Himmler. In 1937, Himmler would state in a speech about homosexuals, "Unfortunately, we don't have it as easy as our forefathers. The homosexual...was drowned in a swamp. That wasn't a punishment, but simply the extinguishment of abnormal life. It had to be got rid of, just as we pull out weeds, throw them on a heap, and burn them. It was not a feeling of revenge, simply that those affected had to go...I have now decided upon the following: in each case [of homosexuality], these people will naturally be publicly degraded, expelled, and handed over to the courts. Following completion of the punishment imposed by the courts, they will be sent, by my order, to a concentration camp."[13]

Homosexuals would be shipped to concentration

---

12. Plant, R. (1987). *The Pink Triangle*. Mainstream Publishing.
13. *Homosexuals & the holocaust*. Himmler Speech on the "Question of Homosexuality." (n.d.-b). https://www.jewishvirtuallibrary.org/himmler-speech-on-the-ldquo-question-of-homosexuality-rdquo

camps and marked with a pink triangle on their uniform. The presence of this pink triangle "outed" these prisoners and made them subject to horrific abuses. "The fate of the homosexuals in the concentration camps can only be described as ghastly. They were often segregated in special barracks and work details. Such segregation offered ample opportunity to unscrupulous elements in positions of power to engage in extortion and maltreatment."[14] Many of these gay prisoners were subjected to castration, or became the subject of gruesome medical experiments which attempted to "cure" their homosexuality.[15]

Concerning the Von Fritsch affair: this incident is true to history as it is described in the novel. "The blackmailer had confused Baron von Fritsch with a retired cavalry officer named Achim von Frisch. Quick research confirmed the egregious error: von Frisch looked like his commander and even wore the same kind of coat. But it was too late...Heydrich's position had been badly damaged in the process. His policemen had appeared stupid, vicious, and dishonest, some had shown divided loyalties, and he himself had lost any pretense to soldierly solidarity with the military, becoming indelibly identified with the 'dirty business.'"[16]

Concerning Axel's statement on Heydrich being accused of having Jewish blood: this rumor was indeed widespread, so much so that it remains to this day. The source of this rumor came from one of Reinhard Heydrich's distant, non-blood relatives possessing a Jewish

---

14. Kogon, E., Norden, H., & Kogon, E. (1960). *The theory and practice of hell the German concentration camps and the system behind them.* Berkley Publ. Corps.
15. Heger, Heinz, et al. *The Men with the Pink Triangle: The True, Life-and-Death Story of Homosexuals in the Nazi Death Camps.* Haymarket Books.
16. Dougherty, Nancy. *The Hangman and His Wife: The Life and Death of Reinhard Heydrich.* Knopf Doubleday Publishing Group. Kindle Edition.

sounding surname. "Ernestine Heydrich…married a Protestant locksmith, Gustav Robert Süss, who was thirteen years her junior and just nine years older than her eldest son Bruno [Reinhard Heydrich's father]. In subsequent years, it was Süss's Jewish-sounding family name that would fuel speculation about Heydrich's non-Aryan ancestry, even though Süss himself was neither Bruno's father nor of Jewish descent."[17] This rumor was further spread by a disaffected pupil of Bruno Heydrich: "The original entry on Heydrich…had been altered by Martin Frey, a former pupil of [Bruno] Heydrich's who had been expelled from the [Heydrich] Conservatory, in a targeted act of revenge."[18]

As a child, this rumor would result in Reinhard Heydrich being relentlessly bullied for his perceived Jewish heritage. As an adult, the rumor would eventually lead to an investigation being carried out by Achim Gercke, head of the Nazis' Information Office. "Scarcely two weeks later, on 22 June, Gercke responded with a detailed report on Heydrich's ancestry and confirmed that he was 'of German origin and free from any influence of colored or Jewish blood'. Gercke insisted that the 'insulting rumor' of non-Aryan ancestry was entirely unfounded."[19] Despite this, rumors of Heydrich's Jewish ancestry persist even to this day.

Concerning Alice's backstory: in the aftermath of the assassination of Heydrich in 1942, the Nazi Party, dazed and thirsty for blood, decided to enact a mass campaign of "reprisals" against innocent civilians to deter future acts against the Reich. Lidice, targeted due to a rumor that one

---

17. Gerwarth, Robert. *Hitler's Hangman: The Life of Heydrich*. Yale University Press. Kindle Edition.
18. *Id.*
19. *Id.*

of the assassins had received aid from the small Czech village, became the most infamous example of this cruelty when it was razed to the ground by the Nazis on June 10th of 1942. "Male inhabitants were herded on to the farm of the Horák family where they were successively shot in groups of ten. All in all, 172 men between the ages of fourteen and eighty-four were murdered in Lidice on 9 June. The shootings were still under way when the first houses were set on fire. By ten in the morning, every house in Lidice had been burned down and their ruins blown up with explosives or bulldozed to the ground. The women of Lidice were deported to Ravensbrück concentration camp while their children underwent racial screening."[20]

A small number of these children were deemed "Germanizable" due to their blond hair and blue eyes. These children were kidnapped into Germany, redistributed to German families, and forced on threat of death to abandon their Czech heritage. The other children of Lidice who "failed" the Germanization tests were deported to Chelmno concentration camp and killed on arrival. Only 17 children from Lidice survived the war.

Concerning Stefan's statement on Himmler's 'weirdness': Himmler was, indeed, enthralled by the paranormal, and every one of the odd things that Stefan thinks of in this section are actually true. "Himmler frequently held 'conversations' with what he believed to be the spirit of Heinrich the Fowler and declared that he received 'advice' from the man he believed to be his own ancestor. He was fond of saying 'in this case King Heinrich would have acted as follows.'"[21]

---

20. Dougherty, Nancy. *The Hangman and His Wife: The Life and Death of Reinhard Heydrich.* Knopf Doubleday Publishing Group. Kindle Edition.
21. FitzGerald, Michael. The Nazis and the Supernatural: The Occult Secrets of Hitler's Evil Empire (p. 133). Arcturus Publishing. Kindle Edition.

A note to my readers

Thank you for reading! If you enjoyed this book, please tell your friends. I'd love to hear your thoughts on *The Hangman's Master*, and reviews help authors a great deal, so I'd be very grateful if you would post a short review on Amazon and/or Goodreads. If you'd like to read more stories like this and get notifications about free and discounted books and short stories, follow me on Facebook, Amazon, and sign up for my newsletter at elysehoffman.com! You can also follow me on Bookbub!